LARRY 3D

Adam Millard is the author of twenty-nine novels, seventeen novellas, and more than two hundred short stories, which can be found in various collections, magazines, and anthologies. Probably best known for his post-apocalyptic fiction, Adam also writes fantasy/horror for children, as well as bizarro fiction for several publishers. Adam lives in Newcastle-under-Lyme with his wife, Dawn, and their two cats, Butter and Toast.

LARRY 3D

ADAM MILLARD

A CIP catalogue record for this book
is available from the British Library

ISBN: 978-1-7384764-6-6

Crowded Quarantine Publications
124 Dimsdale Parade West
Newcastle-under-Lyme
Staffordshire
ST5 8DU

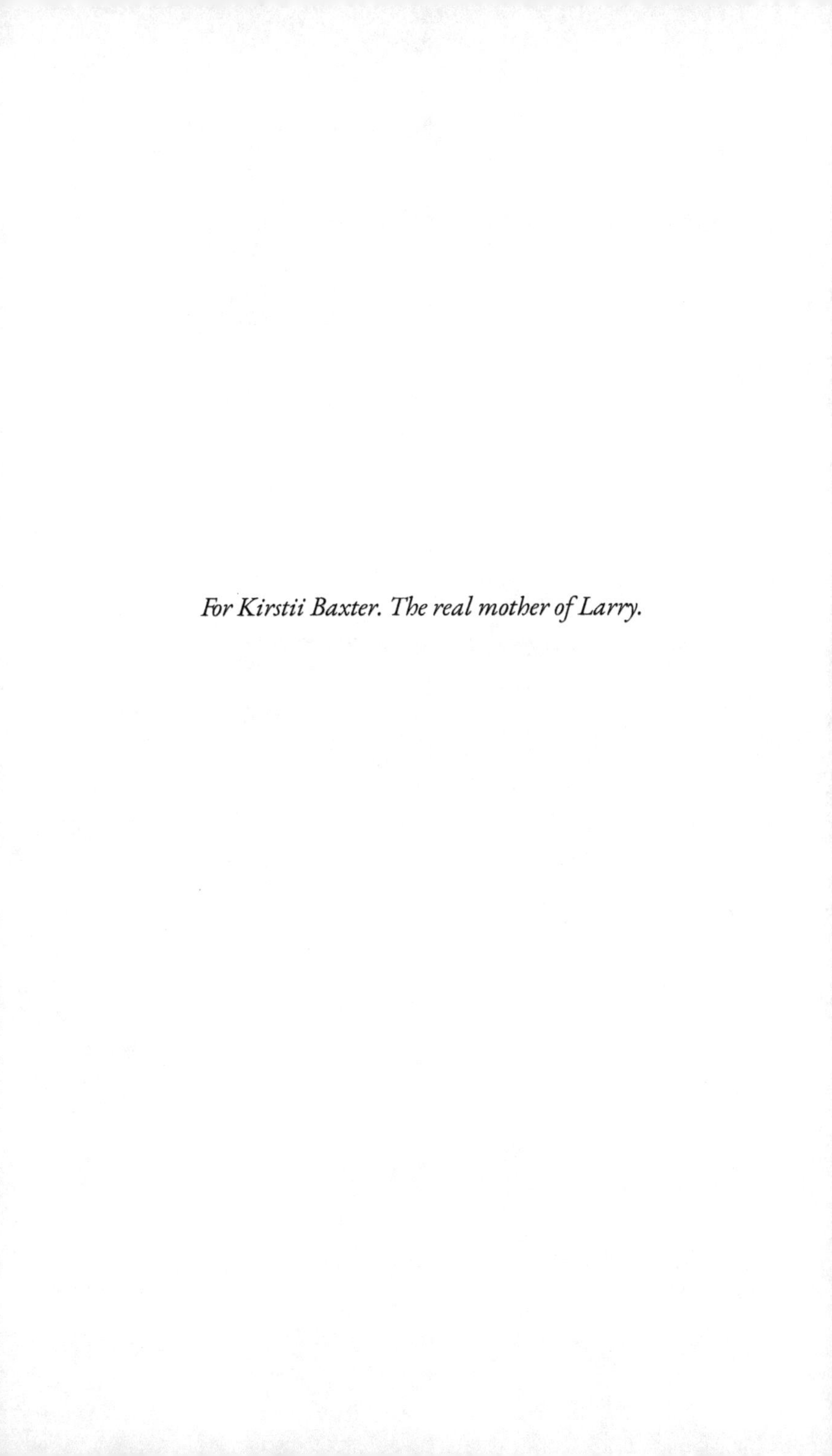

For Kirstii Baxter. The real mother of Larry.

"Part Threes are usually shit. Good job I'm here to make sure this one is more Dream Warriors than Poltergeist III."

- Larry 'Pigface' Travers

ONE

"Pinhead, Freddy, Chucky and the Tall Man all walk into a bar. Sensing danger, the bartender skedaddles. Freddy turns to Chucky and says, 'Fucking hell, you ginger midget, you could have toned it down a bit'." Hank Pleasance laughed maniacally, as he always did at his own jokes. So heartily did he laugh that his cheeks reddened and he began to pass wind. Freya knew he was passing wind because he'd crossed his legs, as he always did when he passed wind. "You get it? It's because he's ginger, and also a midget."

Freya Lee Curtis nodded. "Yeah, Hank, I get it. I just don't think it's funny." And it wasn't. There was nothing funny about ginger people or midgets, even when you combined the two.

"Shit, babe, lighten up," Hank said, still chortling to himself. "Why do you always have to defend ginger midgets?"

"I don't," Freya said, lighting a cigarette. "In fact, that was the first time."

"Look, if you want to fuck a ginger midget, that's fine with me. Just say the word; I've got plenty of girls lined up for me. I had an email just the other day from a hot wife in my area. Horny as hell, she was, and experienced. All I need is a webcam and a credit card…" Hank trailed off there as the queue began to move forwards. When it came to a grinding halt three feet later, Hank continued. "What I'm trying to say, Freya, is that this boy's got options. Granted, most of them are over fifty, and at least one of them I think has a dick, but they're options all the same."

Freya sighed. This relationship was going nowhere—she had known it ever since Hank professed his love for *Amityville Dollhouse*—and at the end of the weekend they would, like Brad and Angelina before them and Adolf and Eva before them, be over. The only difference was, if Hank decided to shoot himself on Sunday, Freya wouldn't be ingesting poison alongside him. There weren't many things she wouldn't put in her mouth, but Cyanide was certainly on the list. Cyanide and avocado.

"Are we ever going to get inside?" Hank stepped out of line for a moment to get a better look at the theatre entrance. "There's a guy up front dressed as Chucky. You want me to bring him back here so you can straddle him?"

Just two more days, Freya thought. Two more days and she could shake free of this imbecile for good. It wasn't fair for her to do it now, before FearFest 2017 had already begun. Hank had paid for the tickets. That would be like severing a dude's head just in case he turned into a zombie at a later date. No, she would wait until the curtain fell for the final time on Sunday. Until then she would put up with his terrible jokes, his appalling flatulence, his propensity to use big words in order to sound smarter than he actually was, even though he didn't know what they meant.

"Ah, I think the queue's about to start coagulating again," Hank said. "Thank God for that. I thought we were going to die of preponderance out here."

Idiot, Freya thought. And as if that wasn't quite enough: *Fucking idiot.*

*

"This is going to be awesome!" Marcia Hodder said. "Do you have any idea how long I've waited for this convention? Do you? DO YOU?"

"Calm your tits, Marcia," said Cynthia Price. "I'm sure it's going to be great, but you don't have to go all Annie Wilkes on us."

"Leave her alone, Cynthia" said the final element of their trio, Aretha Cushing. To Marcia she said, "Go wild, girl. It's going to be a great weekend. I hear there are going to be loads of special guests. That weird bug-eyed little fella from *The Human Centipede 2* is supposed to be here."

"O-M-G!" Marcia said, enunciating each syllable for dramatic effect, and also to make sure she spelt is right. "I love that creepy little fucker. Are you thinking what I'm thinking?" She licked her lips seductively.

"What?" Cynthia asked. "Try to get an autograph?"

"Try to *fuck* him," replied Marcia. This was met with various exaggerated sounds of disgust, but Marcia didn't care. The guy was a film star; it didn't matter if he looked like the bastard lovechild of Marty Feldman and a walrus. He was famous, and famous people are rich. "Besides, he's kind of cute."

"In the same way the baby from *Dead Alive* is cute?" Cynthia said. "Seriously, girl, we need to find you a nice boy, before you end up popping your cherry to Michael Berryman."

Marcia didn't have time for boys. The thought of being tied down to one for any longer than was necessary made bile rise in her throat. "Not interested," she said, running a hand through her jet-black hair.

"Oh, that's right," Cynthia said. "You're saving yourself for Corey Haim."

"Corey *Feldman*," Marcia corrected. Although, if Corey Haim were to somehow claw his way up to ground level, she wouldn't say no. So long as he washed his penis first.

"Whatever," Cynthia went on. "Point being, you're not gonna fuck anyone at FearFest because that's not the kind of girl you are. You're a Final Girl if ever I saw one. No sex, but at the end of the day you'll still be walking around while the rest of us are decapitated and spread about the place like Halloween props."

Aretha nodded. "It's nothing to be ashamed of, Marcia," she said. "Final Girls are awesome. Laurie Strode? Marybeth Dunston? Sidney Prescott? I wish I had the self-discipline you do. Alas, like Cynthia, I'm far too slutty to be a Final Girl. I gave two blowjobs on the way over here."

"You only live two blocks away," Marcia said.

"Exactly. I'm not proud of myself, but these guys were so sweet. And grateful, too. They said they would prefer a BJ to a dollar. I don't look at it as sucking two homeless guys off; I look at it as saving two dollars." She picked something from between her teeth and sprinkled it onto the pavement.

Marcia glanced down at the ticket in her hand. FearFest 2017 – Admit One. It was going to be an amazing weekend of gore and chills. She slipped the ticket into her purse and took out a packet of mints. "Please have one of these," she said to Aretha.

*

At the front of the line, Billy Englund's heart raced. He was nervous, and with good reason. The convention organisers had been watching him for the last half-hour, dubious sideways glances that told Billy everything he needed to know.

They were going to fuck with him.

At four-foot-nothing, Billy Englund was by far the shortest person in the line. So short was Billy that the person behind him—a heavy-set guy dressed as Butterball from *Hellraiser I* and *II*—had taken to balancing his soda on top of Billy's head. Billy had wanted to complain, but it simply wasn't worth it. And besides, every now and then he would catch a whiff of Pineapple Fanta, so it was swings and roundabouts.

"Next!" The woman blocking the theatre entrance was dressed in all black; black tee, Kevlar vest, utility-belt, as if she had a second job right after this one taking on shit that Snake Plissken was too pussy for. A semi-covert earpiece had been pushed into her lughole, and a microphone was wrapped around her face as if she might belt out a Britney song unannounced.

Billy took a tentative step forwards, tripped over the bottoms of his Good Guy dungarees, and face-planted into the door supervisor's crotch.

"At least buy me a drink first," said the lady, pushing Billy's head away before appraising him once again. "You're a little one, ain't you."

"Especially in the trouser department," Billy said, though for the life of him he didn't know why. He was nervous, and when he was nervous he said stupid things.

"You do know this convention is for grown-ups only?" said the lady. "The Pixar convention is next week."

Billy took a deep breath. He knew this was going to happen. It always happened. No matter where he went people mocked his height, or lack thereof. "I'm thirty-eight-years-old," he said, pulling out his ID and showing it to her. She dismissed it with a wave of the hand.

"Anyone can forge an ID these days, little man," she said. "And by the way, did you know you have a can of Pineapple Fanta balancing on your head?"

"It smells nice," said Billy. "Look, how am I going to prove to you that I'm old enough to come in? I don't have my birth certificate on me, and my chinchilla ate my passport."

"In that case, Willow, I'm going to have to ask you to step aside and let these regular-sized people past. This queue ain't getting any shorter, and the first film starts in less than an hour."

"What about if I show you the colour of my pubes?" It was a long-shot, but needs must. "It's like a mini Gandalf down there."

The lady shrugged. "Sure, why not. This introduction to your character has been going on for far too long already. Let's get it over with."

Billy unclasped his Good Guys dungarees and pulled his *Thundercats* briefs to one side. "See? I'm probably older than you. Look at the state of it?"

"It's like Morgan Freeman got tangled up with Brian May," said the lady, squinting at Billy's crotch with no small amount of fascination. She straightened up, motioned for Billy to redo his dungarees. "Okay, well, I guess there's no arguing with that. You're clearly old enough to get in, and also in need of a good willy doctor." She snatched the ticket from Billy's hand and stepped aside. "May you have a wonderful weekend, and if you need anything—a step for the toilet, perhaps, or a periscope—come and find me and I'll see what I can do. My name is Jackie Haig. If you can't find me, find anyone wearing a red tee-shirt. They're the convention redshirts, and it's their job to make sure you have a good time."

"Thanks, Jackie," Billy said, stepping past her.

For a moment, Billy thought the security lady was going to pat him on the head ("*Good little man!*") but she didn't. She removed the Pineapple Fanta and handed it to its rightful owner, the next man in line.

Into the convention Billy Englund went, beyond proud of his Chucky cosplay and the fact he'd made it past security without the organisers offering him a lollipop.

*

Towards the back of the queue stood a portly man dressed as Freddy Krueger, who looked more like a potato that had been left in the microwave for too long than the Springfield Slasher. The razors on his gloved fingers were floppy, made from plastic, purchased from a pop-up dollar Halloween store nine months prior to the event, because this Fat Freddy was nothing if not punctual.

Todd Tony had been a fan of Freddy Krueger for as long as he could remember. There was something about Freddy which separated him from the ten-a-penny slashers ubiquitous in the eighties and nineties. Where Michael Myers or Jason Voorhees silently stalked their victims, Freddy wisecracked them to death. He was funny, and creepy as hell at the same time. Todd hoped that when he died, he would come back as a sleep demon, just like his idol.

"Who's you meant to be, then?" The voice startled Todd; he had been in world of his own. He turned around to find a short woman—older than time itself, or at least Clint Eastwood—staring back at him from beneath a dark hood. Her grin, Todd thought, might once have contained teeth, but not anymore. Black gums, like top-and-bottom slugs, glistened in the early morning sunlight.

"I'm the bastard son of a hundred maniacs," Todd said.

"What, like Donald Trump?" The woman cackled. She would have made a pretty good Disney villain. Todd half-expected her to whip out a poisoned apple.

"Freddy Krueger," Todd said. "You know? The Springfield Slasher, AKA Frederick Charles Krueger, AKA pizza-face, AKA—"

"You's a virgin, aintcha?" hissed the woman, shaking her head. "Bastard son of a hundred maniacs, indeed. When I was your age I was working sixty-hour weeks, trying not to get blowed up by the Germans. And I'd also shagged a dozen men, some of 'em German. That's how you don't get blowed up by 'em."

Todd didn't know what to say to that, so he changed the subject. "Who have you come as?"

"What? You don't recognise me? I'm Edie Travers, mother to Larry 'Pigface' Travers. My Larry would give your Freddy nightmares any day of the week."

Now that the woman had said it, Todd realised how good her cosplay was. She looked just like the woman who had given birth to Pigface. It was uncanny. If he didn't know any better, he would have said it really *was* her. "Is that the film you're here to see?" he said. "I hear it's in 3D, which is cool, so long as it's that good 3D, and not the one where they occasionally jab something out at the audience like they did in *Friday the 13th Part Three*."

The woman grinned, flashing her blackjack gums once again. "It's certainly going to be… an experience," she said. "My Larry would have loved to see himself on the big screen."

Does this woman actually believe she's Edie Travers? Todd thought. Maybe she was senile. Or perhaps she just liked to get into the character once the hood was on. A method cosplayer.

"I'll bet your Larry never contemplated being portrayed by Willem Dafoe, though," Todd said, playing along.

"Who?"

"The actor playing Larry in the film," Todd said. "He's Willem Dafoe, one of the greatest actors never to win an Academy Award. Also, he gets his knob out more often than should be allowed. Maybe that's why he's not yet won an Oscar."

"This Willem Dafoe?" said the old woman. "He's not one of these crazy actors, is he? Like Nicolas Cage or Dennis Hopper?"

Todd laughed. "Dafoe is the king of OTT!" he said. "He's chewed more scenery than Cage, Hopper, and Pacino combined."

The woman visibly deflated. "I 'ope he don't fuck up my Larry's reputation. It took him ages to get the respect he deserved as a much-feared backwoods slasher. I'd 'ate it for some thespian to come in and put the mockers on 'im."

"I'm sure he will do your Larry justice," Todd said. The queue had begun moving forwards. "He was good in *Antichrist*… got his knob out in that one… and *Body of Evidence* with Madonna… got his knob out in that one… and…"

TWO

Inside the theatre, people ambled back and forth across the foyer, spilling popcorn as they tried to grab a quick chat with the directors and producers in attendance or the stars of the films themselves.

"This is madness," Freya said. "I thought it would be busy, but I didn't expect it to be *this* busy."

"They're showing a previously unreleased cut of *The Shining*," Hank said, motioning to a twenty-foot poster suspended from wires above them. "It's a 90-minute Director's Cut in which Shelley Duvall's character has been completely edited out and Jack Torrance, who only gets custody of Danny on the second and fourth weekends of the month, decides to whip the kid up to the Overlook for a bit of father-son time."

"Sounds a bit far-fetched," Freya said. "But if all evidence of Wendy has been edited out, I'm up for it. What time's that one showing?"

"All day in Screen 237," Hank said. "It's normally just Screen 2, but they're getting in the spirit of things."

Freya took out her purse and began riffling for change. She was already hungry, and she'd be positively skeletal by the end of the day if she waited for Hank to buy her a hotdog. He didn't like it when she ate junk food but, come Monday, she would be able to eat whatever she liked. A life of tacos and burgers and cheese awaited her. She didn't care if she got fat. As far as she was concerned, she was losing a hundred-and-eighty-two pounds in one day on Monday. Not a bad start.

She set off for the concessions counter without saying a word.

"Hey, where you going?" Hank called after her.

She pretended she didn't hear him, made her way past what she assumed was not a genuine killer leprechaun, and got in line behind three girls who couldn't seem to make their minds up about which flavour of ice cream to get.

As she stood there, Freya watched the weekend's trailers play out on a large screen to her right. Many of the films she had seen before. *Night of the Living Dead*, the original 1968 classic. "They're coming to get you, Barbara," and all that jazz. It was a movie that held a dear place in Freya's heart, and one she returned to every Halloween. The next trailer was for the Director's Cut of *The Shining*. Jack Nicholson going all kinds of crazy—something he was extremely good at—in a secluded hotel. What's not to like? Trailers for *Psycho, An American Werewolf in London, The Thing*, some Japanese film with one of those long-haired girl-ghosts crawling out of an electrical appliance, and *Poltergeist* all followed. Then there were the reboots. They had remade *The Babadook* for the American market, just because some fans had found it difficult to understand the original's Australian dialect. They had rebooted *Rosemary's Baby* for the new generation, only now it was called *Rose's Babbie*. There were remakes of *Jaws, The Descent*, and *The Fly*, only now there were called *Teeth, Six Girls in a Nasty Cave*, and *Musca Domestica* (because Latin has the propensity to make anything sound scary, even the word 'housefly'). And of course there was *Larry 3D*, the film based upon the life, death, and subsequent reanimation of Larry 'Pigface' Travers.

This was the movie most of those in attendance were looking forward to the most. Freya certainly couldn't wait to see Willem Dafoe's portrayal of the porcine-obsessed lunatic. And luckily, she didn't have long to wait as it was one of the first movies of the weekend.

Squeee! indeed.

"Grab me some nachos, would you, babe?" Hank had sidled up alongside her, much to the chagrin of those waiting patiently in line behind. "And a bucket of coke. I'm thirsty as hell."

Sighing, Freya reached into her purse for more money. Monday, in that moment, seemed a long, long way off.

*

Sitting at the edge of the room, behind tables laden with glossy photographs and movie stills, were the celebrities of the event. Wally Perkins, FearFest's founder and organiser, walked down the row, making sure the celebs were happy and offering to fetch them water and snacks.

Wally Perkins was the kid who got bullied in school for wearing black fingernail polish and drawing metal band logos on any surface flat enough to do so. Not a lot had changed in the past thirty years. Wally was older, but he still wore the black fingernail polish, and he still liked to scrawl the Megadeth insignia on toilet walls whenever he got the opportunity. But he had made a success of himself, which was more than could be said for most of the pricks in his graduating class.

He had created FearFest.

The most successful horror convention in the world.

He had spent his entire life building something from nothing, and it was paying off. Horror films were everything to him. He liked them all, even the really bad ones with Ryan Phillipe in. God, that guy sucked worse than Josef Fritzl's housecleaner.

"Mister Phillipe, can I get you anything?" Wally said. "A bottle of water, perhaps?"

The former actor and Reese Witherspoon-fingerer glanced up from his table, a slight smile playing about his face. "You recognised me?" he said. "You know who I am?" He seemed happy about it. Years of obscurity had apparently made him a little paranoid.

"There's a poster behind you with your name on it," Wally said, motioning to said poster. "By the way, I loved you in *I Know What You Did Last Summer*. Any plans for a sequel?"

"They already made, like, ten of 'em," Ryan Phillipe said. "There was *I Still Know What You Did Last Summer*. Then there was *I'll Always Know What You Did Last Summer*. After that there was *Seriously, I'm Fully Aware of What You Did Last Summer*. Then there was *Dude! Last Summer? Really?*. Then came—"

"Never heard of them," Wally said. He didn't have time for this. "So is that an ixnay on the aterway?" Pig-

Latin was one of Wally Perkins's greatest superpowers. Unfortunately, it wasn't one of Ryan Phillipe's.

"Excuse me?"

"Water? Do you want it or not?"

"I'm fine at the moment," Ryan Phillipe said. "But if you know of any good hostels in the area, I'd be extremely grateful if you gave them a call and asked if they had room for a former Hollywood superstar—"

Wally was too busy laughing to hear the rest, moving along the row of tables to the next celebrity.

CGI Zombie #3021.

Wally had never seen a CGI zombie in the flesh, or the pixels, or whatever the hell it was made of, but it was absolutely terrifying. Black ichor seeped from its flapping jaws, and half its face was off, revealing a chipped skull just beneath the surface.

"Can I get you anything?" Wally didn't know what to call the thing. Did he call it CGI Zombie #3021? Was that too formal? Perhaps he should go for something a little friendlier, a little more casual. "A glass of water, Cee-Gee, or a sack of popcorn?"

The computer-generated model—whose main role had involved running through a street after Brad Pitt, while Brad Pitt tried desperately not to get any dirt in his hair—grunted and swatted several CGI flies away from its face. "Brains?"

"Not today," Wally said. "Only do brains on a Tuesday." Which was a lie; they never did brains. The whole chain of theatres would come under scrutiny if they did. "Maybe we could fold you some hotdogs up to look like brains."

CGI Zombie #3021 shook its head. "Just a glass of water for me, then, thanks."

Wally was slightly taken aback. "Wow! You talk really well! Better than Ryan Phillipe, even."

"Of course I bloody well do," said CGI Zombie #3021. "I used to be a CGI John Gielgud, but there was more money in being a zombie. Plus, one rather enjoys chasing after Brad Pitt, if you know what I mean." It winked and licked its bloodstained lips.

"Not a clue," Wally said. "Anyway, I'll be back with your water in a moment." As he walked away, he watched as CGI Zombie #3021 attempted to pick up its signing Sharpie, only for its hand to go straight through the pen over and over.

Why the fucking hell did it want a glass of water if it couldn't even pick it up? Sometimes Wally despaired. He really did.

"Excuse me, are you the organiser?"

Wally turned to find nobody there. Of course, this well-worn trope didn't last long as something latched on to Wally's trousers and gave them a tug. Looking down, Wally saw the little bug-eyed guy from The Human Centipede II. "I am the organiser," Wally said. "Could you not grab me by the crackers? It might look a little bit strange to people without context."

"I think I've just blocked up three of your toilets," said the diminutive actor. He looked slightly ashamed, though not all the way.

"I'll get one of our redshirts straight on it," Wally said.

"My name is Laurence R. Harvey," said the strange little person.

"Yes, I know who you are," Wally said. "I booked you for the event."

"Not to be confused with the handsome actor, Laurence Harvey, from *The Manchurian Candidate* and *The Alamo*."

"Pretty sure no one is going to confuse you with that man," Wally said.

"That's why I put the 'R' in there," said the actor.

"I think you'd get away with not using the 'R'," said Wally. "Since Laurence Harvey, the handsome one, died in 1973. It's not as if you're both knocking around the convention circuit, is it? Not like one of his fans is going to come up to your table, get your signature and have a little chat, and then go home only to find out they've been duped."

"I like the 'R'," said Laurence R. Harvey. "It stands for ROFL."

"I thought it was Robert?" Wally said.

The tiny star nodded but didn't elaborate.

"And on that note," Wally said, "I'll go arrange for your shits to be removed from three of our toilets. Do let me know if you need anything—"

"Toilet paper," said the actor. "You didn't have any. Had to use a sock." He held up said sock, and that was the moment Wally Perkins decided to never invite Laurence R. Harvey (not Laurence Harvey) to guest at FearFest ever again.

*

She had seen people with axes buried in their heads. She had witnessed her son doing things that no mother should ever have to witness. She had seen black magic in action, that terrifying Voodoo Hoodoo that witchdoctors get up to when they're not out shopping for albino body parts. She had seen all of that, and yet what was going on inside the theatre she now found herself in turned her blood to mercury.

People were dressed as their favourite maniacs, proudly swinging hatchets and stabbing at the air with rubber knives. Edie Travers didn't know what was going on over in the corner, where a small contingent of what appeared to be gremlins were high-fiving on another.

"Madness," she said, turning around and around on the spot, taking it all in. "Absolute madness!"

This was what the world had come to. People were now actually celebrating gore and murder, so much so that entire conventions were dedicated to it. Her son's years of hard work, of butchering innocent teenagers up at Camp Diamond Creek; of traipsing through the surrounding woods for hours on end, looking for something to stick an axe in, and this was what it all came down to.

FearFest.

Edie didn't know whether to laugh or cry.

She looked up to the ceiling, to where a gigantic Pigface mask swung to and fro. It brought back so many memories, most of them fond, some of them a little bit on the weird side, but memories nonetheless.

Here was Larry trying on the mask for the first time. There was Larry making his first kill. Here he was again, running through the trees, a-squeeeing and generally making a nuisance of himself, his trademark axe swinging around and around.

"Ah," Edie said, dabbing a tear from the corner of her eye.

That was why she was here today, why she was putting herself through this nonsense. Larry's last escapade had seen him dead once again, something which he really needed to work on if he wanted to get a reputation as, what they called in the business, a franchise-success. Dying was all well and good, but there would come a time when he'd have to try *not* dying. Edie wasn't getting any younger; she wouldn't always be around to bring her son back from beyond the grave.

Smiling up at the huge Pigface mask, she said, "But today, son, I'm here for you. And these fools haven't a clue what's about to happen." She cackled. So loudly that everyone in the theatre fell silent. All eyes turned to the hooded witch at the centre of the foyer as she screeched and guffawed. It took her a moment to realise everyone was staring at her, and when she did she shrugged. "What? I'm being a movie monster. Isn't that what we're doing here?"

One person began to applaud, and then a few seconds later another. Before long, everyone in the foyer was clapping Edie Travers.

"She's just like a real witch!" said one man.

"She's the best Edie Travers cosplay *I've* ever seen," offered another, though she was also the first Edie Travers cosplay he had ever seen, so the praise was about as valuable as a signed Rolf Harris doodle.

Edie took a bow. These people really were idiots. Idiots who, by the end of the day's festivities, would be hacked limb from limb.

Not long now, son, she thought. *Not long now at all.*

*

"What a crazy old bag," Cynthia said. "It's surprising that they let her in here. Who knows what she's capable of. I hope they've given her a damn good pat-down."

"Sheesh, Cynthia," Marcia said, slurping from her Sprite. "Why do you have to always be so mean? That's somebody's grandma, somebody's mother. How would you feel if it was yours?"

They moved across the foyer, away from the concessions counter. "If that was my grandma," Cynthia said, "I'd have to give my granddad a slap. I mean, just think about it. Having that cackling crone bouncing about on top of you? Granddad's got serious issues."

Aretha shook her head. "I think you're just worried," she said. "Worried that you're going to turn out just like her when you're old."

"Oh, pur-lease," Cynthia said. "I could never turn out like that. I'm gonna be a glamour nana, like Helen Mirren or Judi Dench."

"You're gonna be a regular old lady, just like the rest of us," Marcia said, flicking a piece of popcorn into her mouth. "It's bingo and pant-pissing for you, I'm afraid."

Cynthia turned away, focused on the hooded old lady standing at the centre of the foyer. There was no way on God's green earth she would end up like that, some live-action fairy-tale hag; she would kill herself first. Eat her own poisoned apple just to put herself out of her misery. Just thinking about it made her blood boil. How dare Marcia and Aretha compare her to such a filthy geriatric. How fucking dare they!

"Watch this," Cynthia said, before setting off towards the crazy old bat. Behind her, her friends protested, begged her not to do anything silly. But they were just worried that they might get thrown out of the convention before it had even started.

Cynthia didn't care if that happened. She'd already seen most of the films, anyway. Even the Shelley Duvall-free Director's Cut of *The Shining*, which made no sense whatsoever without the matriarchal element.

She approached the old lady from the rear, knowing exactly what she was going to do. It was the lunatic's own fault for wearing a filthy cloak. She looked like a desiccated Sith Lord.

As she fell in behind the old witch, Cynthia reached down and pinched the dirty cloak between thumb and forefinger, and with one huge yank upwards, it was over the witch's head, and the witch was cursing and howling, and everyone who saw it happen was laughing and snorting and spraying cola from their nostrils, and Cynthia was—for the most part—really pleased with herself. But then she saw the old lady's pockmarked backside, and suddenly she felt very sick indeed, for this particular witch did not believe in underwear, it seemed. Nor did she believe in personal hygiene. Or shaving.

"I think I'm gonna be sick," Cynthia said, hand to mouth, fighting to keep her breakfast down.

The old hag had managed to free herself of the cloak, and was scanning the faces of those around her, trying to figure out which of them was the culprit. "Who did that?" she croaked. "Which one of you little bastards did that?"

"I'm Spartacus!" said some guy who was standing on the other side of the room.

"I'm Spartacus!" a fat man dressed as Freddy Krueger called from the other side of the room.

"I'm Spartacus!" said Ryan Phillipe, jumping to his feet and giving it his all.

"Sit down, Mister Phillipe," said the event organiser, Wally Perkins. "Not even thirty years of acting classes would make you Spartacus."

Ryan Phillipe sat back down, looking more than a little dejected.

Laughing, Cynthia walked across the foyer to where her girlfriends stood. "See? I'm nothing like that witch. I bleach my anus, for starters."

Marcia sighed. "That was really cruel," she said. "I hope she is a witch. I'd like to see her turn you into a frog."

Cynthia grunted. "She's not a witch. She's just some old biddy, out for a break from the care home. Does she look like the kind of person who watches horror films? She's here on the off-chance they'll put on a matinee of *Casablanca*."

"I'll bet she's here for that," Aretha said, pointing up to the cinema lightbox. Labyrinth (U).

"I'll bet she was in it," said Cynthia. "Either that or Bowie still makes the old girl moist."

"Why would they be showing that today?" Marcia asked. "It's not like there's a gore-filled horror convention on, or anything."

"They have to keep the kiddies happy, I suppose," Cynthia said. Although it was a little strange. *Labyrinth* came out in 1986. Why not just go the whole hog and show *Bedknobs and Broomsticks*? "Anyway, I need to piss before the first film comes on. What is it, anyway?"

"Larry 3D," Marcia said. "The one based on real events."

"Aren't they all?" Cynthia said. "Don't go in without me. I won't be a minute. Unless it turns into something else, then just wait a bit longer."

She made her way across the foyer, crunching popcorn into the garish carpet beneath her feet. As she reached the toilets, she noticed that the event organisers had changed the signs for the convention. Instead of a silhouetted woman, there was now a gorgon head, and on the other door there was a Sellotaped picture of legendary horror actor, Bruce Campbell. Beneath Campbell's face were the words, "This toilet's for boomsticks only."

"Cute," Cynthia said. She pushed open the door to the ladies' room—now gorgon's room—and headed on in for what would hopefully only be a number one.

THREE

It was, Wally Perkins thought as he looked down at his watch, time to get things rolling. The foyer was teeming with excited fans. Some had really gotten into the spirit of things, dressing up as their favourite characters from horror films, TV, and even videogames. The event was already shaping up to be the most successful yet, and it wasn't even lunchtime.

And now the fun was about to begin in earnest.

Wally took to the front of the room, one-twoing into a microphone and wincing as it sang back at him with feedback. "One, two. One, two. Testes, testes, Nazi-party, clunge."

Heads turned in his general direction, and voices lowered to an anticipatory whisper.

"Ladies and Gentlemen," Wally said, pushing himself up onto the concessions counter and knocking over a bag of popcorn and a bucket of coke in the process. "First of all, for those that don't know me, my name is Wally Perkins, founder of FearFest."

A cheer went up around the room. Wally pretended not to enjoy it, dismissing the audience's praise with a wave of the hand. When the crowd calmed down once again, he continued, ignoring the chunks of popcorn stuck to the bottom of his six-hundred-dollar brogues.

"Boy, do we have a great event in store for you. Twenty-five films, some of them world premieres. We've got the very first showing of *Larry 3D* in just over thirty minutes' time—"

"Squeeeee!" said one person in the crowd, and then they were all at it. *Squeeeing* and *soueeeing* and snorting like starving piglets.

Wally waited for them to fall silent again before going on with his spiel. "That's right. Not only do we have Larry in glorious 3D, but we have a whole host of classic horror films lined up, as well as several subpar remakes which I know you're all going to hate—"

"Boo!"

"Hiss!"

"Fuck remakes!"

"I actually quite liked the *Evil Dead* remake—"

"Shut the fuck up, dickhead! No one did!"

"Feisty crowd," Wally said. "That's what I love about the horror community. You're all just so… quarrelsome."

"Fuck you!"

"No we're not!"

"We are a bit!"

"Shhhhh…"

Wally decided to change the subject; this was getting him nowhere. "Not only are we showing a shitload of movies you've probably already seen a hundred times and are only here to see again because the studios have added an extra frame-per-second, or some shit like that, but if you look to your left, you'll see a whole plethora of film stars and authors from the world of horror—"

"Holy shit, is that Ryan Phillipe?"

"Thought he died?"

"You suck, Ryan Phillipe!"

Ryan Phillipe stood up, gave the tough crowd a nervous wave, and sat back down again.

"Who's the guy with the poo sock?"

"That's Laurence R. Harvey."

"Not to be confused with Laurence Harvey, the dead film star."

"Oh."

Wally tapped the mic with his palm, and all faces turned his way. "Yes, well, I think you'll agree we've got quite a celebrity turnaround, given our limited funds. Ryan Phillipe is doing this just to get off the street for a few hours, isn't that right, Ryan?"

Ryan Phillipe, in the middle of unfurling a filthy sleeping bag, nodded.

"And, if you prefer your movies stars to be of the digitally-enhanced kind, right at the back there we have one of the stars of *World War Z*, CGI Zombie #3021."

The audience turned just in time to see CGI Zombie #3021 salt-and-peppering his own arm. Where he'd procured a digital pepper-grinder from was a mystery. He gave the crowd a shy wave before resuming the seasoning of himself, flickering in and out of existence like a malfunctioning hologram.

Wally made his way to the other side of the concessions counter, being careful not to slip on its coke-slick surface. "Over here, we have a bunch of authors whose names I can't remember. Blah-blah Hawkins, something-something Bradshaw, the guy who audaciously uses the name Stephen King on Amazon, even though he's shit… just shit… at everything he does."

"You're not the real Stephen King!"

"Yeah! Stop it!"

"Even your grocery list has errors!"

"Asshole!"

Perhaps, Wally thought, I shouldn't have introduced that guy at all. "Okay, can we show a bit of respect to our guests, huh? They've come a long way. I'm pretty sure, as horror authors, if they'd wanted to be insulted they would have just stayed at home. Now, we have roughly twenty minutes until our first screening, so if you want to get refreshments, now is the time. We have a whole host of overpriced goodies for you right here at the concessions counter. Want a coke? Ten dollars. Hotdog? Hope you've re-mortgaged your house. Ice cream? I'll give you three grand for your firstborn, and a grand for every extra kid after that." He laughed, even though he wasn't joking. Not even about the kids. "So, after three, I want you all to give me your best scream Queen scream. Can you do that?"

"I guess."

"I wasn't planning on being part of the show."

"Does Ryan Phillipe have to do it?" asked Ryan Phillipe.

"On three," Wally said. "One… two… three!"

The foyer was filled with shrill screams. Wally Perkins fell backwards off the counter, such was the power of the combined screech. The microphone picked up the words, "… my fucking back," as Wally climbed to his feet and made his way—limping—to the other side of the concessions counter.

When the squeals died down, Wally said, "I want you all to have a great time this weekend, but I also want to remind you that this is a no-smoking, no-blowjob, no-piddling-in-the-aisles cinema chain, and we have to respect the venue as much as we respect Christopher Lee, or Ti West, or Uwe Boll… okay, maybe not Uwe Boll. What I'm trying to say is we'll be back next year so long as you guys behave yourselves."

Mumbles echoed around the foyer. The old hag—Wally didn't know the lady, but he'd been watching her throughout his speech—made her way to the ladies' toilet.

"I want to thank each and every one of you for supporting this convention," Wally said. "Whether it's your first time, or your tenth. It means a lot that we get to put this whole thing on every year, and we wouldn't be able to if it wasn't for you guys. So, thank you."

Cheers.

Applause.

So excited was he that the guy dressed as fat Freddy puked up in his own popcorn. He put it in the bin, for he wasn't a complete monster.

"Without further ado, Ladies and Gentlemen, get yourselves to your respective screening. Starting right now are *Larry 3D*, *The Shining* (now with 100% less Shelley Duvall), *Psycho, Musca Domestica*, and *Night of the Living Dead*."

Another round of applause. Fans checked their tickets, made their way from the foyer towards their movies.

I fucking love this job, Wally thought. *Also, I think I've broken my coccyx.*

FOUR

The flusher was broken. Cynthia couldn't believe her luck, for she had just laid down foundations large enough to support the Taj Mahal. "Goddammit!" she said, yanking at the chain once again, hopeful and yet resigned at the same time. "Seriously?"

There was only one thing for it. Walk out of the cubicle, head held high, and pretend it was someone else's.

She did just that, and as she exited the stall, she came face to face with the woman she had only recently publicly ridiculed. The *Disney* witch, right there, standing at the mirror trying to make herself look pretty.

"That smell you?" asked the woman.

"Somebody else," Cynthia lied. "Can you believe that? Somebody did a nasty shit, broke the flusher, and then left it for someone else to take the blame. It looks as if I'm the patsy."

"It looks as if you've taken a nasty shit and broken the flusher," said the old lady.

"Woman," Cynthia said. "I don't even know you, but you're extremely rude."

The witch turned, and her eyes were filled with malevolence. And also some kind of putrid gunk that Cynthia wanted to point out but didn't have the balls.

"You're the bitch what pulled up my robe, aintcha?" the woman said. "Put my innards on show for all and sundry?"

Cynthia smiled. Why should she be afraid of this geriatric coot? She was about as menacing as her own grandmother, Ethel Price. The woman was a simpleton. The doctor had informed Ethel Price that she had Alzheimer's and cancer, and a minute later Ethel Price had said, "Well at least I don't have cancer." This was kind of the same.

"I didn't do anything of the sort," Cynthia said. "And also, you've got some really nasty gunk in your eye. You might want to scoop it out."

"SILENCE, WHORE!" It came out of nowhere, which is where it should have stayed, as far as Cynthia Price was concerned.

"Now just you wait a minute," Cynthia said. "You don't know me. What makes you think you can talk to me like that. In fact, you know what, I don't need to stand here and take that sort of abuse. I'm walking out of this smelly toilet, and I'm going to make sure you get ejected from the convention. You're off your tits, lady. Madder than a box of frogs. Crazier than a zebra in a horse race. More mental than Jim Carrey on LSD—"

"Ouch," said the old witch.

"Ouch, indeed," Cynthia replied. "And if you must know, it *was* me that exposed your hairy asshole. It was me, and I don't care. People need to know what it is, what it looks like under there. You're a monster! A monster!"

The witch reached into her cloak, pulled out an axe and grinned. "Do you know who I am?" she said, grinning with dark back gums. "Do you think I'm here to watch stupid horror films?"

Cynthia shook her head. "Well *now* I don't," she said. "Now I think you're one of those crazy theatre people. The ones who just like to show up with a weapon and ruin it for the rest of us."

"Actually," the witch said, "I'm the mother of Larry Travers. This isn't just cosplay. I'm the real one. I pushed him out of my body, fed him on these wrinkled old titties for almost ten years. I'm Edie Travers, the real one, and I'm going to bring him back. And you're going to help me."

"I am bloody well not!" Cynthia said, taking a step towards the door. The witch blocked her exit, slashed at the air with her axe. "Okay, I can see that you've got issues, lady. I know a good psychiatrist, and also a great arse-shaver. I can help you. There's no need to cut anyone HEEEELP!"

"Nobody is going to help you," said the old lady. "If you're lucky, I'll get your carotid. It'll all be over in a couple of seconds. If you struggle, well, it might take a bit longer."

"You're crazy!" Cynthia couldn't believe this was happening. She had never seen the Shelley Duvall-free cut of *The Shining,* and now there was a possibility that she never would. "Please, just let me go. I won't tell anyone that you're off your head. Or that you think you're the real Edie Travers. This'll be our little secret. Like the time I lezzed off with my cousin. Or the time I put the kitchen window through with a soccer ball and then blamed it on the next-door neighbour. Nobody needs to know about this."

"You're right," said the witch. "Now, let's get a wriggle on. We have to be in the projection room before the film starts, otherwise it won't work." She swung the axe through the air, slashing Cynthia across the cheek; blood spattered across the mirror. Cynthia squealed. It was all very dramatic, like something from *Downton Abbey* or

Midsummer Murders. "You're going to bring my Larry back from the dead. It's a dodgy premise for a part three, but I reckon it'll work."

"No!" Cynthia screeched. "It's a terrible premise for a part three. Please, just—"

The witch brought the handle of the axe down on top of Cynthia's head, and suddenly everything went fuzzy and dark. But it wasn't quite enough, and consciousness returned a second later.

"Oh," said the old axe-wielding bag.

Raising a hand to where the axe handle had caught her, and giving it a quick rub whilst hissing through her teeth—because everyone knows that helps with the pain—Cynthia said, "Oh? You donked me on the head with an axe, and all you can say is 'Oh!'?"

The axe came down again, and this time the impact of its wooden handle dropped her to her knees. Blackness.

White stars at the back of her eyelids.

Then she came to, her knees soaked with lady-piss, for these toilets hadn't been mopped in hours. "Seriously?" she said. "Two attempts?"

"You're not right," said the old lady. "You must have a high tolerance for axe handles, or summat. I walloped you as hard as I could that time, as well—"

"I know you did!" Cynthia said. "I saw the cords in your neck bulge."

"Give me one last try," said the witch. "And if it don't work this time, I'll letcha go and pick someone else."

Cynthia frowned. Blood dripped from the top of her nose and plinked into the pee-puddle beneath her. "One last go," she acquiesced, bowing her head forward to make it easier for the old lady. "But seriously, you fuck it up, I'm getting up and walking out of here, and you're getting reported to the theatre staff for brutality and attempted murder. Deal?"

The witch nodded. "Keep still. I think that's why it din't work last time. Your head was wobbling all over the place. Reckon I—"

"Just do it already," said Cynthia. The first two hits had failed to render her unconscious; however, they had made her slightly retarded, simple enough to allow the witch to have a third bite of the cherry without putting up a fight.

The witch raised the axe and Cynthia closed her eyes. And then it struck her how surreal this whole thing was, and that she was allowing this old lady to repeatedly smack her with the handle of an axe. There was something not quite right about that. It wasn't something she would normally allow. In other words, Cynthia realised—perhaps too late—that her brain had been irreparably fuddled.

"Wait a second," Cynthia said. "I—"

This time, unconsciousness came. Not only did the lights go out, one of her eyes did, too. And a couple of teeth. And the bit of tongue at the end that you always bite into when you're hungry and going hell for leather at a pizza crust.

The last thing Cynthia heard was the sound of her own bladder giving way. That, and the witch's maniacal cackle.

*

Billy Englund made it all the way to the double doors of his chosen screening, *Larry 3D*, before being accosted by a member of security once again. He wouldn't have minded, but it was the same one who had given him grief at the entrance. What did she say her name was? Haig? Jackie Haig?

"If it isn't my little friend," she said, patting the top of his head. "Billy, isn't it? That's right. Billy. So, what do you think of the con so far? I'll bet it looks a little different down there, huh? A lot more crotches in your face than most of us are getting, huh?"

Billy nodded. Although, he didn't know how many crotches Jackie Haig had had in her face that morning, so it was pure conjecture.

"Going in to see this one, huh?" she said, motioning vaguely to the doors behind her. Doors through which people were walking. Doors through which Billy should have been walking, and yet wasn't because of the giant security guard standing in his way. "*Larry 3D*, huh. The one with The Pigface."

"Actually it's just Pigface," Billy said.

"Oh, so the 'The' is silent, huh?" said Jackie Haig. "Like The Batman and The Carrie?"

Billy shook his head. "It's just Batman," he said. "There's no 'The' in Batman, and Carrie was just the girl's name. Why would a girl put 'The' at the front of her name?"

"It worked for The Queen," said Jackie. "She's rich as all hell, now. Doubt it would be like that if she'd just gone with 'Queen'."

"Can I go into my film now?" Billy had had enough of this asininity. He just wanted to get his 3D glasses—special ones which he'd had to order in advance due to his petite stature—and watch the fucking movie in peace.

"Sure," said Jackie. "Actually, I'm on a break now for a while. No more people getting in here without my say so. So I thought, why not check out a movie. And then I thought, I'd really like to see that one with The Pigface. I wonder if little Billy Englund would like to sit next to me. And then I thought, of course he would. I'm a whole lotta woman. More woman than he ever did have. And so here I am. I'm just a six-foot security guard, standing in front of a three-foot-nothing Chucky, asking him to love her." She erupted with laughter.

Billy nervously did the same. Was this a come-on? Was this giant coming onto him? God, he hoped not. She could literally eat him for breakfast and use his stripped bones to pick her teeth.

"Did you ever see that movie?" she said, settling down a little. "*Notting Hill?* Now *that* was a damn fine movie. It had The Julia Roberts in it—"

"Can we just get this over with?" Billy said. It was his turn to motion to the doors behind her.

"Sure thing, honey-midget," Jackie said. "After you." She stepped aside, but Billy went through her legs anyway. It was easier that way, and cut at least three seconds off his journey time.

*

"Are you scared?" Hank cracked open a bottle of beer which he'd manage to smuggle in past security. He chugged it, dropped the empty onto the floor, and proceeded to open a second.

"Why would I be scared?" Freya said, watching as people continued to file into the theatre. "It's just a film. A film with actors, created by producers and directors and first grips, and best boys, and those people who run off to get coffees. It's just special effects; latex and appliances and squibs and rubber axes. There's nothing to be scared of."

Hank's mouth had dropped open, and he stared at her as if he couldn't believe what she was saying. Eventually he said, "Way to spoil the atmosphere. It's not just a film, though, is it? This one really happened."

Freya had read all about the murders up at Camp Diamond Creek. She had seen the newspaper articles about how, all those years later, he came back for more, despite being old enough to watch *Little House on the Prairie* without feeling guilty. She had seen the news reports about how he was still alive, somehow, and tearing through Haddon like a whirlwind, chopping people up like Patrick Bateman having a seizure. She had seen all of that, and yet this film version they were about to watch just didn't seem right. It was far too Hollywood.

"The only thing I'm scared of," Freya said, "is Willem Dafoe getting his dick out."

"I've heard he does it in every movie," Hank replied. "Even when you're not seeing it on screen, it's right there, just out of shot. That's why Tobey Maguire always looked a little flustered when they were doing a scene together. Dafoe's meat-puppet was right there, pointing at Maguire like something that just burst out of John Hurt's stomach."

"Hm," Freya said. "Well, hopefully this will be one of the times he keeps it off-screen. I'm feeling a bit queasy as it is without being confronted by that."

"Imagine!" Hank said. His breath was already beer-rancid, and a fleck of his spittle landed on Freya's lip, which she quickly wiped away. "Imagine it in 3D! Can you imagine? A big 3D Willem Dafoe dick coming toward you at a hundred miles an hour?"

Bile rose in Freya's throat. *If I'm sick,* she thought, *I'm going to make sure it goes all over him. All over.*

"I heard Dafoe did all his own stunts for this one," Hank went on. "Like, there's this scene where Larry blows up in a toilet. And that's actually Dafoe under all that fire. That's his real flesh just melting away."

"Bullshit," Freya said.

"Seriously!" Hank replied. "He's one of those, what do you call it when an actor really wants to get into a role so he puts on six-hundred-pound or starts walking around the set with a poo in his knickers?"

"Method acting," Freya said.

"That's it. He's a method acting… he's one of those, a method man."

The theatre was almost full. People were making their way to the last few available seats. An anticipatory mutter thrummed all around the room.

The calm before the storm, Freya thought, though quite why she thought that, she didn't know.

It was, after all, just a film.

With actors…

By producers and directors…

With grips and best boys and…

*

Marcia sat there on 13J. It was the very same seat which had once been frequented by Joan Rivers, Ted Cruz, John Wayne Gacy, though the theatre tried to keep it a secret as no one wanted to think they were touching something that had also touched Ted Cruz. Marcia was comfortably oblivious of the fact.

"I wonder what's taking Cynthia so long," Aretha said, licking her lips and snapping her compact shut. "She's going to miss the start of the film."

"We did tell her we'd wait for her," Marcia said. "She's probably looking for us."

"You think we should go back to the foyer?"

"No," Marcia said without any hesitation whatsoever. "She'll find us."

It was much nicer when Cynthia wasn't around. Marcia and Aretha were closer. If Cynthia were there right now, she'd be saying nasty things about Marcia, and sometimes Aretha would stifle a laugh. There was nothing mean about Aretha, but when Cynthia was there she changed a little—just an inch to the right, but it was noticeable, and Marcia didn't like it one bit.

"What if she's stuck in the cubicle again?" Aretha said, clearly unable to put Cynthia out of her mind. "She might die in there. Remember last time? She ate seven of her false nails before someone rescued her."

"Can we *forget* about Cynthia just for now?" She didn't intend it to come out so mean, and yet there it was, tinged in vitriol and dripping with spunk. "She's a grown-ass girl. If she can't even go to the toilet on her own, then she deserves to perish."

"I know she can be nasty to you," Aretha said, "but she doesn't mean it. It's just the way she is—"

"She's a cunt!" Marcia said.

Three rows in front of them, a fat guy dressed as Freddy Krueger turned around and asked, "Who's a cunt?"

"Mind your own business, Fat Freddy," Aretha said. "Jeez, can't you call a woman a cunt anymore without some obese dream-demon getting involved?"

"Look, I'm sorry," Marcia said, rubbing her friend's arm. "I know you and Cynthia get on, but I don't like her. I never have done and I never will. If something really terrible was happening to her right now, right this minute, I wouldn't care."

Aretha smiled a little. "I'm sure you don't mean that," she said.

Oh, I mean it, Marcia thought. *I mean it so hard.*

FIVE

"Did you sign anything?" Ryan Phillipe stood from his table in the foyer and stretched his arms above his head.

"A couple of things," said CGI Zombie #3021. "Well, I would have if I was a corporeal entity and not just a collection of highly-intricate pixels. Can't even pick the bloody pen up. A few people wanted selfies, though, so that's cool." It nodded and peeled a hunk of loose flesh away from its face. Digital blood rained down onto the foyer carpet before disappearing completely. "What about yourself? Much business?"

Ryan Phillipe shook his head. "I don't think anyone remembers me," he said. "One girl came over thinking I was Justin Timberlake, but when I told her who I was she fucked off."

"Harsh," said CGI Zombie #3021. "On the bright side, at least you're not that guy." It pointed across to where Laurence R. Harvey sat, swinging a poo sock.

"I wish I was him," Ryan Phillipe said. "At least he has a poo sock."

The foyer was still teeming with fans, but a lot of the attendees had gone off to watch films. It was going to be a quiet couple of hours. Ryan Phillipe didn't know whether to head to the bar, try to use his Hollywood status—what was left of it, anyway—to bum a few drinks. With a bit of luck the bartender would be female.

I'll pretend I'm Justin Timberlake, he thought. *If it gets me a couple of shots and a pint of IPA, I'll even sing Cry Me a River.*

*

With the girl over her shoulder, Edie Travers left the Gorgon's Room and stepped out into the foyer. There were a lot of people out here, milling around with no real agenda, but they all seemed to be so entrenched in their own silly lives that they didn't notice her

But that all went tits up a second later when the event organiser (Wally something-or-other, Edie thought)

popped up like an impatient waiter at an all-you-can-eat buffet.

"What's going on here?" said Wally. "You appear to have a girl across your shoulder. An unconscious girl, at that."

"It's me cosplay," Edie said, thinking quicker than she ever had before. "It's just me cosplay, dearie. I'm Bill Cosby. Ain't nothing more 'orrific than Bill Cosby."

Wally frowned. "But you're an old white lady," he said.

"I ain't gonna black up, am I? What you think I am? Some sort of fuckin' loonie?"

The organiser seemed to consider Edie's unlikely story for a moment before motioning to the girl stretched across her shoulders. "She looks very real," he said. "She's breathing, and there's a lot of blood coming out of the top of her head."

"All animatronics," Edie assured him. "It's amazing whatcha can do these days with a gallon of pig's blood and a PhD in engineerin'."

"You have a PhD in engineering?" Wally's frown returned with a vengeance.

"Got three of 'em," Edie said, shifting the girl from one shoulder to the other. She wasn't getting any lighter, that was for sure. "Now, if you'll excuse me. She might very well look like she don't weigh much, but it's 'er innards, you see. All clockwork an' wires an' unleaded petrol. Weighs a fuckin' tonne, she does."

"Well," Wally said, stepping aside. "I'm sorry to have kept you. And please make sure you come to the cosplay competition this afternoon. There's a very good chance you'll win with your 'Bill Cosby carrying an unconscious girl' design."

As she shuffled away, muttering expletives to herself, the girl across her shoulder began to moan. Edie turned around to find Wally staring at her, a dubious expression painted across his face.

"Just 'er sound system," Edie said. "Dolby 5.1, and all that malarkey." The girl continued to groan. "Sometimes you just have to give 'er a little *thwock* on the noggin." She took out the axe and did precisely that. The girl fell silent once again, though her legs and body continued to twitch intermittently. "See?"

"Have a lovely day," Wally said with a smile, and with that he turned and marched across to the box office, no doubt to tally up the final takings.

Edie turned and continued toward the projection room, where the magic (don't expect too much detail, because that would spoil the illusion) would happen.

Not long now, Larry. Almost there.

*

As the lights in the theatre began to dim, a cheer went up around the audience. Some people applauded, whilst others thought it was a good time—and how could there ever be a *bad* time?—to toss their snacks up into the air, showering everyone in the vicinity with popcorn rain and nacho cheese hail. The curtains at the front of the room, which was undeniably the best place to put them if you wanted them to cover the screen, began to slowly open. The anticipation was palpable. You could have cut the atmosphere with a spoon, and other things to that effect.

Billy Englund was nervous for a very different reason. The huge woman sitting beside him was definitely trying to get into his *Thundercats* pants. Every now and then she would reach across and squeeze his leg, and every time his leg would shoot up into the air involuntarily. Jackie would laugh, and Billy would pretend to laugh, because that's what you're supposed to do when someone twice your size playfully squeezes your leg. But inside he was crying. Inside his soul was withering. Inside he—

"Do you know, short-round," said Jackie. "This is the most fun I've had in a long time." She laughed, so heartily that her **SECURITY** badge fell off and disappeared into the abyss between her legs. "I'm not just saying that because you're disabled, and it's the law to make disabled people happy all the time."

"Hang on a minute," Billy said. "I'm not disabled. I'm short. That's all. Would you say Tom Cruise was disabled, or Salma Hayek?"

Jackie shrugged. "Well, they're not *normal*, are they? I mean, if you saw one in the street, you would do a double-take. Let me put it another way; if you had a cannon, it would be rude not to fire them out of it toward a Velcro dartboard."

"Probably would be a bit rude to fire Tom Cruise out of a cannon just because he's short." Billy could see he was getting nowhere. The security lady clearly had one or two reasons to discriminate against people of short stature. Probably because she had never been less than five-foot-tall in her entire life. Jackie Haig had probably landed on the wet, bloody floor of the delivery room wearing a black bomber jacket and smoking a roll-yer-own.

"I'm sorry if I offended you," she said, squeezing his kneecap once again, which sent the entire limb into spasm. "Who am I to stereotype someone because of their height, or in your case lack of? I'm built like a brick shithouse. I haven't taken a shower in almost three years because the cubicle in my bathroom is too small. I wore a yellow coat the other day and someone climbed on my back and asked me how much it would be to the station."

"That's awful," Billy said, yawning. "Any chance we can watch the film in peace? I've been looking forward to it for a very long time—"

"I heard Willem Dafoe's in it," Jackie said. "Great actor. Strange penis."

"Shhhh." Billy pointed toward the screen. The previews were over, and titles were beginning to form. "It's about to start."

Jackie squeezed his leg one last time before pushing a pair of 3D glasses up the bridge of her nose and settling back into her chair. The person sitting behind was about to complain, saw the size of the woman responsible, and decided that it had been a while since they had last visited the emergency room, anyway. No harm, no foul.

SIX

A girl runs through the woods, squealing, sobbing, and making far more noise than one would expect from a girl trying to avoid confrontation with an axe-wielding maniac. She's beautiful. Impossibly beautiful. The kind of beautiful you see on shampoo bottles and Pornhub. She's topless, for some reason or other, and she's very well-endowed. She's not the Final Girl. That much is obvious. She's fodder. She's been fucking or drinking or smoking weed, and now she's going to be punished by Pigface, the porcine-masked lunatic currently one step behind.

She trips and falls, eats a mouthful of dirt before scrambling to her feet once again. She sets off, only now she's limping, because she's done herself a mischief. All in all, it appears she's having a bit of a shocking night.

She rounds a wooden cabin—the kind of place you'd normally find a mass-murderer lurking in the shadows, but this girl's no genius, and so she plods on implacably, closer to death with every step she takes—and then she sees it.

And then she screams.

Hanging upside down from the corner of the cabin is a boy. He's not handsome, not anymore, not now his face has been peeled away. He looks like one of those things you see in kebab shops, the rotating things with the meat on. He looks just like that, except he's wearing trousers, and everyone knows doner meat doesn't care for fashion.

The girl screams again.

The camera cuts to our killer. His axe is bloody, and so is his apron. He looks like a demented butcher, if said butcher liked to wear the heads of his victims. Upon hearing the scream—which isn't difficult, since she's apparently trying to contact the afterlife—Pigface changes direction.

A title card appears on screen. CAMP DIAMOND CREEK – 1975. *And then it is gone again, and we cut back to the delirious girl.*

"Bobby!" she's crying, slapping the dead, upside-down boy across the place where his face used to be. "Bobby, wake up!" She punches him hard in the chest, and he swings back, away from her, as if Ali has just jabbed it with all his might. "Bobby! He's coming, Bobby! Pigface is coming!"

Off in the distance there is a shrill squeeeeeee, the favoured war-cry of our titular antagonist. Upon hearing it, the girl falls silent, slapping a blood-drenched hand to her mouth.

Just then, Bobby's dead body swings back and hits her, knocking her away from the cabin. It's a silly bit of slapstick, but for some reason it works.

Then Pigface is there, rushing toward the girl with his axe raised and—is that his penis, windmilling as he runs across the undergrowth? Strange, but okay. It's an odd-looking penis, not unlike Willem Dafoe's. The girl doesn't see it; she is far too busy tripping over things which aren't there, hiding behind trees far too slim to conceal her, and whimpering so loud, anyone this side of Maine can probably hear her.

In other words, she's doing all the things expected of beautiful fodder, and she's doing them well.

"Squeeeeee!" wails Pigface. He's put his willy away now, perhaps satisfied it's been seen by at least one person. Unlike Jason Voorhees and Michael Myers and Cropsey, Pigface likes to run, and he's shifting now in his pursuit of the girl. If physics existed in this world, he'd already have caught her three times, but where's the fun in that?

Cut back to the girl, who has stumbled upon some kind of barn. In she goes—which is what we've come to expect from our beautiful fodder—and no sooner is she in than she's burying herself with straw.

Pigface arrives, and his mask is all lopsided because he's been going hell for leather and that's what happens when you wear an ill-fitting mask and sprint with it on. After bumping into a few things—racking, the long-dead remains of an Impala, a bright yellow sign which says CAUTION—he steps on a rake, and its handle springs up to smack him in the snout.

Slapstick use #2 is a complete failure. It's like something out of a Laurel and Hardy film. Perhaps it would work better in monochrome. Probably not.

Cut to the girl, beneath the straw. She's whimpering like a farting baby, but in her own head she probably thinks she's silent.

Fodder.

Meanwhile Pigface, who has now recovered from the comedy rake to the face, is turning the place upside down in his search for the girl. "I know you're here!" he says. "Pigs have an excellent sense of smell. Did you know that? Shit eyesight, but we can pick out a grain of salt from a hundred yards away." He throws a toolbox across the room.

Cut to the girl, who is now shaking so badly that her earrings have fallen out. Maybe she finally realises that hiding beneath a layer of straw was a bad idea, after all. Probably not.

Pigface, realising that all he's checked everywhere BUT the trembling pile of straw at the back of the room, turns his attention to it now.

"Ahhh," he says. And, "Squee-diddly-dee," because apparently the producers hired Seth McFarlane to write the script.

He makes his way toward the hay, whistling a tuneless ditty as he does so.

The girl is now shaking so much, there is barely any straw covering her. We can see her legs, kicking like beached fish, but it seems our killer can't, unless he's playing along.

"This little piggy went to market…"

Oh, so we're going to do that now, are we? Why not. In for a penny, in for a pound.

"This little piggy stayed at home…"

The girl, finally deciding she's a sitting duck, leaps up, but by the time she does, Pigface is right in front of her, axe raised, mid-

"Squeee!"

The axe comes down, buries itself in the top of the girl's head. Her scream, frozen in time, becomes nothing more than an agape mouth and a river of piss trickling down the inside of her leg. It's an unfortunate way to go, but let's be honest: she was fortunate to make it this far.

After a few seconds, she slumps to the ground, the axe still deep in her cranium, and it takes Pigface an age to yank that thing free.

"Come on!" he says, pulling and pulling and pulling. It's just like the thing with King Arthur and the sword in the stone, except there's a lot more blood here. "For fuck's sake, woman! What's your head made out of? Glue?"

It finally pulls free, and Pigface falls over backwards, completes a manoeuvre that Mary Lou Retton would have pulled out of due to insurance purposes, and lands in a heap on the floor of the barn.

Camera pans out.
Pigface says, "I'm too old for this shit."
Fade to black.
And not a moment too soon, as far as some critics are concerned.

SEVEN

William Naughton (Bill to his friends, Billy to his mother, and Darkvader666 to his email list) had been a projectionist all his life. There was nothing else he would rather do. The compactness of the booth—you couldn't swing a cat, and William had tried on several occasions—and the smell of the celluloid gave him a semi-on, which was remarkable considering his age.

His booth was decorated with vintage film posters. Here, a Turkish-language *Evil Dead* (*Kötü Ruh*), there a German *Jaws* (*Der weiße Hai*). It was his haven, a home away from home. He took better care of the booth than he did his own apartment, because if you don't have pride in your work, you might as well call it a day.

For William Naughton it was all about the classics. A huge fan of the Italian cannibal films of the seventies and eighties, he had once carved off a small portion of his own arm and cooked it, just to see what all the fuss was about. Tasted a lot like chicken, in fact. Gristly chicken. Chicken which had just got off a treadmill.

These new films, with all their 3D technology and 10.1 surround-sound, they just didn't appeal to him. He liked the crackle of old film. He liked the missing reels.

He loved to see Charles Bronson beating seven shades of shit out of some prick thug.

"Take this film," William said, talking to himself as he so often did in the confines of his booth. "This *Larry 3D*. What a pile of utter shit. *Motel Hell* did the pig thing a lot better back in 1980. Hell, even *Porkchop II: Rise of the Rind* is better than this bollocks."

He lit a cigarette, because up here he could do whatever the hell he wanted. Up here in Naughton's Booth, there were no laws other than those he imposed upon himself. Like: no masturbating over Disney films. That was a pretty important one. And another rule: If it's got Adam Sandler in it, accidentally lose the reels. That one is mightily significant, because if you can prevent just one person from having to sit through another awful Sandler film, you're as much a hero as Superman, or Iron Man, or Bono.

William exhaled a plume of grey-blue smoke into the booth and relaxed back in his chair. It squeaked beneath his weight, but it was a sturdy chair, a chair which had once belonged to David Fincher, back when he was a projectionist. Then he'd made *Se7en* and *Fight Club* and the rest, as those with a shitty vocabulary and a propensity to rely heavily upon idioms would say, was history.

But Fincher's old projectionist chair now belonged to one William Naughton (Billy to his mother, Weird Willie to the family in the apartment next-door) and he loved that chair. He made love to that chair—sometimes—and he would marry that chair, if such a thing was feasible.

Down in the theatre, girls screamed and boys chuckled, even though they were just as terrified as their partners. William had been doing this long enough to know that men tried to act tough in front of their dates. They would act tough, and then go straight home to ring out their underpants. So it goes.

Extinguishing his cigarette in an already overspilling ashtray, William pushed himself up from his and Fincher's chair and made his way across to the edge of the booth. There, a red button sat halfway up the wall. He pushed it, and a whir—of mechanisms and cogs and rusty components—echoed around the room. Less than ten seconds later, a minibar appeared, pushing out from the back wall like a tantalising alcoholic shit from a brick-and-mortar anus.

"It's that time of day," William said. "Drinks are on me, and soon to be in me… something or other…" He trailed off there and set about pouring himself a large whiskey. The good stuff, too; not just some over-the-counter pish.

With drink in hand, and a crack-pipe in the other—no rules in Naughton's Booth—he made his way back to the chair and settled in for a pleasant half hour of meditation.

That was the plan. However, when an old hooded woman barged in a second after he had sat back down, a groggy-looking teen stretched across her shoulders like a scarf from the Ed Gein range, he almost dropped his whiskey.

"What the bloody hell are you doing in here?" he asked, pushing himself up from the chair. "You can't come in here. This is Naughton's Booth. *My* booth. *I'm* Naughton. Billy to my mom. Noncey Noncey Naughtonshire to the little bastards at the end of the street—"

The old lady wasn't listening. She was far too busy trying to find somewhere to plonk her unconscious teen. "Out the way!" she screeched, pushing William aside as if it were he that was trespassing. "God, it stinks in 'ere. Whatcha been doin'? Fartin' and wankin' by the smells of it."

William couldn't believe this. This was his sanctuary, and it was being turned over by a batty old twat with a seemingly narcoleptic bird strapped to her back.

"That's it!" William said. "I'm ringing theatre security. You shouldn't be up here, and I'm pretty sure you're up to something devious with that girl, so whatever it is, stop it right this instant." He lunged for the telephone hanging upon the wall, but by the time he got there he didn't have fingers to pick it up. Instead, bleeding stubs pawed at the handset. It took him forever to realise something terrible had happened.

Then the pain hit him, and he turned to see the old lady standing right there, axe in gnarly old hand and black-ichor grin reminding him that he hadn't brushed his own teeth that morning.

The girl was now slumped in his and Fincher's chair, one leg draped over the side. She was still out of it, but appeared to be coming slowly around.

"You… you lopped off my fingers!" William was in so much pain that he had forgotten how to swallow. Thusly, gallons of saliva seeped from his wide open mouth and dribbled down his chin. He was in a fair old state.

"You was gonna ring theatre security," said the old lady. "You was gonna tell on Edie Travers. That's me, that is. I bet you've heard of me, ain'tcha? I bet you know who I is?"

William nodded slowly, for he had heard of her. "You were in… in the film," he just about managed. "Played by… Kathy… Kathy Bates."

The old lady straightened up and lowered the axe momentarily. "Fer fuck's sake," she said. "Is that who they got to play me?"

William nodded.

"All the actresses in the world an' they pick 'er to play me." The old lady clearly wasn't happy with the casting department. "Kathy shagging Bates. Do I look anythin' like Kathy Bates?"

Now, William had learnt this the hard way, but if someone asks you if you think they look like Kathy Bates, the answer is always no. Even if Kathy Bates asks if you think she looks like Kathy Bates, the answer is still no.

"No," William said as he scanned the booth floor in search of his missing fingers. "Nothing like her."

The old lady could not be placated, however. On and on she went, listing hundreds of actresses better-equipped to play her than Kathy Bates. William was too busy cowering and trying to glue his pinky back in place with sheer willpower alone to hear her.

"Anyway, William," the old lady said. "I know this is a bit of a shitter, but me an' the young 'un here 'ave got something we need to be crackin' on with. If you could just put your 'ead on the minibar over there and keep very still, this'll all be over in a jiffy."

William dropped the finger he had been trying to reattach. "You're… you're going to kill me? With that axe?"

"Unless you 'ave a better idea," the old lady said.

William did. He had lots of better ideas. Anything, in fact, was better than having his head removed by what appeared to be a rather blunt axe. "We could pretend none of this ever happened," he suggested. "I could go downstairs, step out onto the street, and start a-running, just like that fella Gump did."

"I'm afraid not," said the old lady. "No, a beheadin' is the only way. Sorry about that."

"Then I shall have no choice but to put up a bit of a fight," said William, adopting the stance favoured by most pre-1900 bareknuckle boxers. "But I must warn you. I have never hit a woman before, and I'm not sure how much I'll be able to hold back."

"What's that over there!" the old lady screeched.

William turned to look in the direction she was pointing, and then something *thunked* into his chest, knocking him back into shelves of canned films. When he looked down, saw the axe embedded in what was, as far as he understood, a pretty vital part of his torso, he turned his attention back to the old lady.

"You tricked me," he said. Now there was more than just drool slipping down his chin. There was blood. Lots of blood. He could taste its bitterness, like sucking pennies—not a hobby of his, but he could imagine that's what it might taste like.

"You were gonna 'it me," said the old lady through a black-gum grin. "A poor defenceless ol' bag like me. I 'ad to protect meself."

Dropping to his knees, William fingered the axe handle. "Should I pull it out? What do I do? I should pull it out, I think!"

"I wouldn't do that if I were you," said the old lady. "You'll only die quicker." She seemed to consider that for a moment before taking a step towards William. "Actually…" She reached down, latched onto the wooden handle with her filthy talons, and snatched the axe from his trunk.

He groaned. Blood pumped from the wound, spraying the booth floor all around him. "What a world," he said, before his eyes rolled up into his face and he collapsed in the blood like a marionette whose strings had been cut.

EIGHT

According to the title card on the screen, it is now 2014. A man who looks suspiciously like Willem Dafoe sits at a table with a woman who looks a lot like Kathy Bates (but don't tell her that, whatever you do). They are eating something that could be stew, could be soup, but is probably neither. Scattered around the cabin are various bones and skin-lamps. It's as if they'd caught Leatherface on a quiet day and asked him for a hand with the decorating.

"You're seriously thinking about going back into the killing game?" the woman who might be Kathy Bates asks. "After all these years, you're gonna don the pig mask and go back out there, hunting promiscuous teens and butchering kids in wheelchairs for no other reason than they're vulnerable and geeky?"

Larry—played here by one of the world's greatest actors, for it is none other than serial flasher, Willem Dafoe—puts down his spoon and turns to the old lady. "I just think I'm wasting my life," he says.

"You've had *most of it!" says the old lady, ostensibly Edie Travers, mother to the titular Larry. "You've killed 'undreds of the little bastards. And now you're in your sixties, you're thinkin' of comin' out of retirement?"*

He's obviously not going to listen to a word his mother says, and he tells her as much. "I'm not going to listen to a word you say, Mother."

She thinks he's being a stubborn little shit, and she tells him as much. "You're being a stubborn little shit, Larry."

"You're just thinking about yourself," Larry says, tearing a piece of bread in half. At least, it looks like bread, but there's a very good chance it's nothing of the sort. "You're just worried that, with me gone, you'll have no one to wipe your arse or wash your dildos."

The old lady clicks her tongue. "I can wash me own dildos," she says. "And, given time, I'll learn 'ow to wipe me own arse. But that's not what this is about. Son, I'm worried about yer. A lot of years 'ave passed since you last went a-killin'. And you remember what 'appened the last time. You got outsmarted by a final girl. You said that was it, that was the end of it."

Larry dips his not-bread into his not-soup and nibbles at it. "I've made up my mind," he says. "It's time to get the old mask out. Time to sharpen the axe. Time to go back out into the world and see what old Pigface can catch."

"Don't talk about yourself in the third person," says Edie. "Only assholes talk about themselves in the third person." She sips at her wine, though there's no way it's wine. The cabin must be miles from the nearest Londis.

Excusing himself from the table, Larry stands and walks across the room, to where his mask hangs from a hat-stand. He tries it on for size, runs through a few 'squeeee's, just to make sure he still has it in him. Turns out he does. He's just as terrifying as he ever was. Maybe even more so, now, because now he's played by Willem Dafoe.

"Please, Larry. Don't do this." His mother is up from her chair now. She creaks, or the chair creaks, or perhaps it's the sound of the audience's cells dying. "I'll die if you do this. I know I will. Mother's not as young as she used to be."

"Don't talk about yourself in the third person," Larry says, and he's clearly pleased with himself.

Edie rushes across to where he's standing, and grabs onto his arm. "I don't want to die!" She's hamming it up, now. There's barely any scenery left; most of it is stuck between her teeth. "You'll be killin' me if you leave, Larry!" It's a performance worthy of an Academy Award, but this is a horror movie, so the chances of her actually getting one are reduced by roughly one-hundred-percent. Kathy Bates or no Kathy Bates.

"You're not talking me out of it, Mother," Larry says. He pulls the mask on all the way now, and for the first time we see him as he is meant to be. His eyes, those evil, malevolent eyes, peering out through those thin slits in the mask are enough to put the shits up anyone. Larry Travers is gone. This is Pigface—Master of

Massacre, Bacon Brute, and Gammon Goremaker—and he's out of retirement.

"So you're out of retirement, are you?" The old lady has stopped begging, and has walked across the room, to where a notepad and pen sit atop a bureau made out of nipples. After scribbling something down, in that angry way people sometimes do, she tears the top sheet off and hands it to Pigface. "That's how much rent you owe me."

Larry pulls the mask off and reads the paper. "Sixty-five grand!" he says, exasperated. "You do know I don't get paid to kill kids. It's not like the last Friday of the month I get a lump-sum."

"Ha!" says the old lady. "In that case, you shouldn't be doin' it. If you can't put bread, or whatever the hell it is, on the table, then it ain't worth the 'assle."

Larry tears the paper in half and eats it. As a statement it is ridiculous, but he is still hungry from not finishing his supper, so it goes down a lot better than it should. When he's finished swallowing, he says, "Maybe I'll start right now." He pulls on the mask once more and picks up the axe. "Maybe I'll start this year's butchering right this minute."

"But The Apprentice is on," says the old lady, motioning to the bone and feather TV sitting at the corner of the cabin. "Right bunch of bastards this year. You'll miss it."

Pigface doesn't care about The Apprentice. He limps across the room—he's had a dodgy back for weeks now, after taking a slip— axe swinging down by his side.

As he leaves the cabin, Edie Travers wails fill the night. And then, as the screen fades to black, she mutters, "Well, that's fucked that, then."

NINE

Cynthia opened her eyes as pain washed over her, a terrible pain, far worse than indigestion or trapped wind. Everything was so blurry, so fuzzy; it was like looking through frosted glass. Frosted glass which hadn't seen a window-cleaner in decades.

I must be dreaming, she thought. She could not remember anything that had come before. It was as if her slate had been wiped clean. Even her own name escaped her.

"Glad to see you decided to join me," said a voice to her right. "I was about to go ahead and perform the reanimation ritual while you was unconscious. Likes a sleep, don'tcha?"

Cynthia blinked away the grogginess and tried to push herself up. Something held her in place. Straps. She was strapped to a chair. *It looks like the kind of chair David Fincher would sit in,* she thought.

"Where am I?" she said, struggling against her restraints. "Who are you? Where am I?" She saw, now, the face of her captor, and it was a face which brought back everything, including her breakfast. "You… you hit me with an axe… several times…"

"Oh, don't keep goin' on about it," said the old lady, who appeared to be sharpening an axe. In the absence of a whetstone, she was rubbing it back and forth across her backside. Sparks were flying all over the place.

"What are… what are you going to do to me?" Cynthia couldn't believe this was happening. To her, of all people. She was one of the most popular girls at school. Even the teachers loved her—especially the male ones. This shouldn't be her, strapped to a chair in a room lined with foreign film posters and celluloid cans. This should be Marcia.

"Don't you worry your pretty little 'ead about it," said the old lady. "Now, I'm gonna start chanting in Latin in a minute, and I don't want any interruptions, is that clear? The thing with Latin is, there's a fine line between reanimating a dead slasher and summoning the Patron Saint of Cheese. The last thing I need is any distractions, you hear me?"

"But I'm supposed to distract you," said Cynthia. "I'm not just going to sit here will you spout off in some dead and creepy language, because whatever its purpose, you can damn near bet it's not going to be beneficial to me."

The old lady shrugged. "It ain't the Latin what'll 'urt you," she said. "It's what comes after the Latin." She raised the axe high into the air, but the booth was only small and plaster rained down upon her. She coughed a little and shook the dust off before continuing. "Now, if you'd 'old still, we can get this show on the road."

Cynthia screamed. Unfortunately for her, she'd screamed at the exact same moment one of the actresses screamed on the film playing in the adjacent theatre. Cynthia screamed again, and was once again matched by the actress on screen. "Fucking hell," she said. "What are the odds?"

The old lady began to chant. "*Vos profundus pinguis cocta potatoes cum illa? Vade et caca in pilleum et ipse traheatur super aures tuo. Mendax mendax tuum braccare flagare.*" Roughly translated, she'd said, "Would you like fries with that? Go shit in a hat and pull it down over your ears. Liar, liar, pants on fire," but Cynthia didn't know that. It sounded so menacing, so terrible. This was Satan's language: "*Erat abhinc viginti annis hodie, Centurio Piper catervam canere docebat,*" if Satan used phrases like, "It was twenty years ago today, Sgt Pepper taught the band to play."

"Please!" Cynthia gasped. "Please stop with the Latin. Don't you know any other languages? Perhaps a nice French? A gentle soothing Afrikaans?"

"Quiet!" the old lady snapped, swiping Cynthia across the face with the back of her hand. "I said no interruptions. You'll put me off me stride, and I'll end up resurrecting Cthulhu instead of me son." She cleared her throat and began once again with the Latin.

This isn't going to end well for me, Cynthia thought. It very rarely did where Latin was concerned.

As the witch continued reciting nonsense, she took something out from underneath her cloak and placed it on the floor in front of Cynthia. It was a framed photograph. In it, a man wearing a pig mask stood next to an ocean. His speedos looked incongruous, considering the mask he wore.

"1979," the old lady said, smiling slightly. "I remembers it well. Larry got the shits that weekend. Had a bad curry, we did." She drifted for a moment, her smile almost beatific. "Anyway, that's enough reminiscing. We ain't got time for a flashback sequence."

She went on with the Latin; Cynthia went on with the sobbing. It had finally hit home that she was going to die. She wasn't terribly keen on the idea.

"*Anulos qui animum ostendunt omnes gestemus!*" the witch said, which in English translated as "Let's all wear mood rings," but she wasn't to know that. The important part was coming up next

"An' that," said the old lady, "is pretty much all the Latin done." She raised the axe and keened like a cat stuck in a chimney.

"Just a minute!" Cynthia gasped. "Please. You don't have to do this. I've got so much to give."

"Oh you are giving," said the witch. "You're giving me back my Larry." She brought the axe down hard.

*

The girl's head split like a ripe coconut. One of her eyes popped out and shot across the room. Her bowels must have given way, for there was an unsightly stench in the booth, and Edie was positive it wasn't her. Though she had been wrong before.

Blood from the girl's gashed head geysered out. Edie was dripping; everything in the booth was red with blood.

Everything except for the framed photograph.

"Shit!" Edie said. "Get some on the picture, you daft bitch, otherwise it ain't gonna work." She grabbed the girl by the hair and yanked her head forward. Blood pitter-pattered down onto the photo. Edie sighed with relief. Everything was going to plan, and Edie said as much. "Everything's going to plan."

Once the picture was suitably crimson, Edie picked it up and carried it across to the rotating film reels. In just a few moments, her son would be resurrected—for the second time. Either that or nothing would happen, and Edie would head back to the cabin in the woods to give her dildos a rinse.

*

Pigface was back. It was official, and he had made it official with the slaughter of a young girl who looked a lot like Jane Levy, the actress. In fact, she was the spitting image of her.

"So that's it, is it?" the old lady says. She's angry. We can see that she's angry because she's got that look about her. You know the one? The look? "You're just using this cabin like a hotel. Coming back here every morning with a bloody apron. Who 'as to wash it? Me, that's who! I'm not your maid, Larry, and this place ain't the Hilton, so I'd appreciate it if you didn't treat it as such."

Willem Dafoe's Larry sits at the table, hollowing out the head of Jane Levy. "Ma, you know how much work means to me," he says, as if his work is no more or less important than, say, delivering pizzas or eating cheese off Chinese people's toes, like those little fish do.

"It's bad enough you're out of retirement, at your age, but do you really 'ave to bring your work 'ome with yer? You're getting grey matter all over me favourite doilies."

Larry continues to work away at the head, cutting slivers off, peeling the scalp back, sucking the wax from its ears with his own mouth. It's disgusting to watch, but it's impossible to look away.

"Why don't you find yourself a nice girl, Larry?" says the old lady. "One what you don't decapitate? You ain't getting' any younger, and it could be the best thing what ever happens to yer."

Larry brings his fist down on the table. Jane Levy's head jumps up and comes back down on its neck stump. "You know I don't get on well with women, Ma," he says. "And by the way, has anyone ever told you how much you look like Kathy Bates?"

"How fucking dare you!" says the old lady. "And stop tryin' to change the subject. You should go the city, find yerself a lovely bit of muff. Give me some grandkids, before I'm too old to give a shit."

"I'm not going to the city, Ma," Larry says. "What do you think this is? Babe II?"

The witch frowns. "Well, you can't just sit here all day, hollering out that 'ead. I've got things to do. You'll a've to go play in the woods, or something."

"*Play in the woods?*" *Larry says. "I'm sixty-odd years old, Ma. I'm not out there, building dens, looking at discarded porn magazines and swinging from ropes." He stands from the table, picks up the Jane Levy head and drops it unceremoniously into a bloody sack, before throwing the sack over his shoulder and grabbing his axe.*

"I want you back for supper tonight," the old lady says. "It's more of that stuff what's like bread."

"Delightful," Larry says. He's making for the door when, all of a sudden, everything turns red.

Blood red.

"What's 'appening!" the witch screeches. She's looking at the backs of her own gnarly hands, trying to figure out why they're suddenly dripping with blood.

Larry turns back in to the room, allows the sack to fall from his shoulder. He's looking about the place, mesmerised by the phenomenon. "I don't know," he says. "It's not you, is it, Ma? Not your time of the month, is it?"

"Cheeky little shit," she says. "No, it's nothin' to do with me. I 'aven't 'ad a time of the month for sixty years. It's blood, though, innit? You know better than I do. It's blood, Larry, ain't it?"

Larry nods. It is blood. Lots of blood. And it seems to be in the atmosphere, floating all around the room. Which is impossible.

Unless this film has a really big budget, like Inception or Spice World.

"So much blood!" Larry says.

"Make it stop!" says the old lady. "It's staining me doilies!"

"Hang on a sec, Ma. I'll just go fetch my magical blood-stopping machine." He shakes his head; blood is dripping from his hair, which is light brown and shaggy, just like Willem Dafoe's. "This shouldn't be happening! None of this should be happening!"

"I know!" says the old lady. "I'm Kathy Bates! Things like this don't happen to Kathy Bates!"

Larry squeeeees.

The old lady screams.

And—

*

—the audience didn't have a clue what was going on.

"What a bizarre film," Billy Englund said, peeling Jackie's hand away from his crotch for the umpteenth time. "I don't understand. Are they trying to break the fourth wall, or something, because they're going about it all wrong? You have to be clever to break the fourth wall. *Fight Club* did it well, and *Funny Games*. Even *Annie Hall* did it better than this."

"What are you talking about, you funny little man?" Jackie Haig was seemingly only interested in on thing. And that thing was a funny little man.

"Are you even watching?" Billy motioned to the huge screen at the front of the room, which was now crimson with, apparently, magical on-screen blood. "These two actors are pretending not to have a clue what's going on. It's desperate. I don't think Kathy Bates has been in anything this bad since *Curse of the Starving Class.*"

"Never mind all that," Jackie said. "I've got a starving ass. You wanna blow this joint and grab a pizza, then maybe back to mine for a quick—"

"I don't like women," Billy said. It was a lie; he liked women a lot. Given the chance, he would date one. "It's not you, it's me… erm, I've got AIDS. Er, and crabs. Fuck it, my crabs have got AIDS."

But even that didn't seem to work. Jackie pulled him up from the chair and practically swallowed his face. For the longest time he could only see the inside of her mouth. And then came the first scream—

*

Marcia had lost track of what was happening up on screen. Willem Dafoe hadn't got his dick out for quite some time, which she was grateful for, but the film just didn't make any sense. Did Kathy Bates just refer to herself as Kathy Bates? Didn't she know how gross that was? Hadn't anyone told her the rule?

"Is this meant to be a comedy?" Aretha said, shovelling popcorn into her face.

"I don't think it knows what it is?" Marcia said. "And where did all that blood come from?" Maybe I fell asleep, Marcia thought. Maybe I fell asleep, missed a bit of a massacre, and then woke up again. That was the only explanation.

"It came out of nowhere," Aretha said. "I really don't get it. Is it trying to be one of those arty-farty Giallo-type films? If someone comes in now, wearing a black glove, we're leaving."

Marcia didn't want to leave. She wanted to see how it all panned out. She also wanted Cynthia to come back from the toilet, for her cola was getting warm. And then came the first scream—

*

Freya Lee Curtis had a bad stomach. She didn't know whether she was going to be sick or be needing a change of underwear, but she felt rotten.

"Are you okay, babe?" Hank whispered. "You've gone ever so pale."

Freya nodded. "I'm okay. Just watch the film." And Hank did just that. Freya, on the other hand, couldn't concentrate. Something had happened that she had missed, because now the screen was redder than the devil's dick. And the actors were running around the cabin, trying to figure out what was going on. It was fairly bizarre.

"You're not up the duff, are you?" Hank said, leaning in again. His breath smelt of beer and chocolate. "If you're up the duff we'll have to get rid of it. You understand that, don't you?

"I'm not up the duff," Freya whispered, embarrassed in case anyone could hear the conversation.

Hank seemed to relax at that. "Whew," he said, wiping invisible sweat from his brow. "That *is* a relief, and it means we can stay together for now." He chugged on his beer bottle; Freya wanted to ram it down his throat. She was about to do just that when the first scream came—

*

Todd Tony scratched his head. He wished he hadn't bothered, because he was still wearing his replica *A Nightmare on Elm Street 4: The Dream Master* glove. Although the blades were plastic, his head was bleeding now, though not nearly as much as the screen in front of him. It was crazy. He had never seen a cinema screen bleed before. Perhaps it was one of those gimmicks, like William Castle used to use in his films.

Castle had had vibrating devices installed in every seat of the theatre for *The Tingler*. There were rumours of *Magic Mike XXL* utilising the same technology, but the clean-up afterwards would have been too expensive.

If this was a gimmick, it was a cheap one. The blood, Todd thought, didn't look real at all.

He was about to say as much to the small guy dressed as Chucky sitting a few seats away to his left, but the poor little bastard was being half-devoured by the female security-guard.

It just isn't fair, Todd thought, settling back in his chair. *Even midgets have a better sex-life than me. I might be chunky, but at least I'm in proportion.* He was still pondering upon the subject—*How do they even manage it? I mean with big people, not people of their own species? And do they have normal willies? Wouldn't it drag on the floor?*—when the first scream came.

*

The first screams all came at the exact same moment in time, shortly before the second scream and a whole second before the third scream, and so on and so forth until the screams all blended into one.; a siren of terror and confusion.

Like at a Yoko Ono concert.

*

Two Minutes Earlier:

Willem Dafoe/Larry drops to his knees. He's clearly in a lot of pain, clutching at his stomach and making gargling sounds, as if he's choking on something other than scenery.

"Larry?" says the old lady. "What is it? What's the matter?"

"I feel like I'm splitting in two!" he says. "Like… like I'm coming apart!"

"You're trying to steal the show, ain'tcha?" she says, shaking her head. Blood flicks in all directions; she's like a sprinkler system directed by Tom Six.

"I'm not," Willem Dafoe/Larry says. "It really hurts. Something's trying to come out of me!"

"Not in here, you don't," says the old lady. "To the bathroom!"

"It's not a shit, Ma," he says. He's now scratching at himself, as if trying to remove the first couple of layers of skin. "Please! You gotta help me!"

The old lady looks confused, and not the least bit concerned. "Maybe it was that bread stuff," she says. "I knew it wasn't bread the moment I dug it up from the pig-sty."

But Willem Dafoe/Larry is no longer listening. The pain is apparently too much. He stands up, sweat pouring from his entire body, pulls his trousers down and howls at the moon—which isn't even out yet. "It's coming, Ma!" he screams. "It's coming, and I can't stop it!"

"You should never try to stop it!" the old lady screams back. "You'll rupture your 'ole—"

"MA!"

"You've got your willy out again," she says. "It's any excuse with you, ain't it?"

"MA!" He drops to his knees, assumes the position most commonly utilised by birthing sheep or… coffee tables. He grits his *teeth, pushes his face forwards for no apparent reason—it is a 3D movie, after all—and says, "Kill me! Kill me noooooow!"*

And then it's all over. Blood continues to swim through the air, a crimson miasma splattering anything it comes into contact with, but that's not the craziest thing that's happened in the last two minutes.

"Squeeeeeee!" says the thing on the floor. Willem Dafoe stands, pulls up his trousers (somewhat reluctantly) and glances upon the thing with those crazy old eyes of his.

"Why's there a piglet on the floor?" asks the old lady. "And why's it growing like that? Piglets don't grow like that."

"I'm Willem Dafoe," says Willem Dafoe. "I'm not Larry. I'm Willem Dafoe." He's still looking at the creature, which is now the size of a five-year-old child or one fifth of a Kareem Abdul Jabbar. "What's going on here? This isn't in the script. I'd never allow for something to pass through my anus, even if it was in the script."

By now the creature is wearing a white butcher's apron. It is clear that this thing isn't a real pig. It's a child—nay, now it's a man—wearing a cheap pig mask. And he's still growing at a rate not seen since Tom Cruise was named as Lee Child's Jack Reacher.

Kathy Bates is running for the exit; it is clear she's seen enough to make an executive decision. And that decision is to get the fuck out of dodge before the pig-man-thing gets to his feet-trotters-things.

But the bastard's up quicker than you can say candied maple bacon, and he's now snatching the axe up from the floor. He holds it out, for no other reason than this is a 3D movie and it looks great to those watching at the local IMAX, and then he brings it arcing around.

"Shit!" Kathy Bates just about manages, and then her head's off, bouncing around the room like one of those balls you used to get when you were a kid. It's a moment of light relief in what would otherwise have been a bit of a brutal scene, and if Kathy Bates hadn't just been decapitated, there's a good chance she would have been offered a sitcom alongside Zach Braff and Aziz Ansari, who would no doubt be typecast as an Indian... again!

"Ma!" Willem Dafoe says. "I mean, Kathy!"

"Squeeeee!" says the pig-man, wiping his axe across his filthy apron. And then, "Hey, you're Willem Dafoe! I've seen your willy." Then he's looking down at himself, confusedly, as if—much like the audience watching back at FearFest—he's trying to figure out just what the hell is going on. "I'm... I'm back!" he says. "How did I get back?" He's asking Willem Dafoe, as if Willem Dafoe has all the answers.

Or any of the answers.

Willem Dafoe shrugs. "You fell out of my arsehole," he says. "This is a film. We were making a film—"

"Who's WE?" asks the pig-man.

"Me and Kathy Bates—"

"Whoa there, Willem!" says the pig-man, recoiling in horror. "You can't just go around saying people look like Kathy Bates. You'll get your ass kicked!"

"You're him, aren't you?" says Willem. "You're the real Pigface? Larry Travers?"

Pigface nods. "What gave it away?" He sarcastically motions to the pig mask, the bloody white apron, and the fact that he's now holding the only piece of ID he's ever owned: a membership card for the local Axe Appreciation Society.

"This can't be real," says Willem Dafoe. "This isn't happening. You're dead. You died back at Camp Diamond Creek, and then again over in Haddon."

"I'm still pissed off about that," says Pigface. "That thing in Haddon really put me on a…" He trails off there, turns to the camera, as if he sees something of interest. "Willem Dafoe, who the fuck are all these people?"

Willem Dafoe now faces the camera. His expression says it all (which is a great thing to have if you're an actor). "Looks like a theatre filled with nubile young teenagers to me," he says. "But this can't be happening. It has to be a dream, or a nightmare, or an episode of Tales from the Darkside, which it can't be because my agent would have told me about it."

But Pigface is far too busy licking his lips now. "A film, you say?"

"Yeah. A 3D film." Willem is clearly still mesmerised by the fact he can see a theatre filled with people, and they're all looking terrified. Especially the Fat Freddy sitting three rows from the front.

Pigface squeees. "If it was a film," he says, "it's not anymore. It's a buffet. An all-you-can-butcher buffet, and I'm hungrier than I've been in a long time." He squeees again, and walks toward the camera menacingly.

Willem Dafoe doesn't know what to do, so he does something very Willem Dafoe.

He leaps onto Pigface's back, wraps an arm around the maniac's throat, and tries to prevent him from killing a bunch of innocent kids.

*

When a twenty-foot Pigface came through the screen with Willem Dafoe riding him like Seabiscuit… that was the moment the first screams sounded around the theatre.

The moment reality and unreality blended into one.

It was a strange time for all involved.

Just like a Yoko Ono concert.

TEN

Freya Lee Curtis was one of the first to her feet. "What the fuck is happening?" she screamed. But it was a stupid question, for it couldn't have been any clearer what was happening. Willem Dafoe and Pigface—the real Pigface, who had slaughtered hundreds of teenagers with an axe—were down at the front of the theatre, wrestling.

Everyone was up now, screaming and shouting and rushing towards the exits. Hank grabbed Freya by the hand, but she snatched it away.

"What's the fucking matter with you?" Hank said. He looked hurt. Offended. And he had a smear of mustard on his lip which made him look utterly retarded. "I'm trying to save your life!"

"Save your own," she said. "I can take care of myself."

Hank apparently didn't need telling twice. He was out of there quicker than Whitney Houston in a bubble-bath.

Down at the front, Pigface and Willem Dafoe were slowly shrinking, returning to a normal size. Willem was ostensibly loath to let the mass-murderer get the better of him, and was holding on as tightly as he could.

Freya pushed her way through a crowd of people. The whole theatre had bottlenecked; it was chaos. Freya thought it was the sound of popcorn crunching underfoot, but when she looked down, she saw faces. Faces of crushed people. Crushed people faces.

Someone had climbed up onto Freya's shoulders, and she turned to find the Chucky cosplayer staring her right in the face. "Sorry," he said. "Too many genitals down there."

"Hold tight," Freya told the little fella. She nudged people aside, for there was no way she was going to die here, not like this, with a midget on her back. By the time she reached the exits, she was covered in sweat. Some of it was even her own.

Out in the foyer the madness continued. A lot of people were already outside; Freya could see them through the glass doors, running for their cars. The building's alarms were now squealing. At least she thought it was the alarms, but then she realised it was the midget on her back.

"Everyone, can we just calm down?" Wally Perkins was up on the counter. "The film can't be that bad. It's got Kathy Bates in it, for Christ's sake!"

A panicking woman dressed as a Cenobite (one of the sexy ones, not Chatterer) pulled Wally down from the counter and screamed into his face, "You can't say that about a person! It's not her fault!" And then she was off again, barrelling toward the doors at full pelt.

Freya didn't hear or see much after that. Unconsciousness can do that to a person. At some point, just before she reached the exits and sweet, sweet freedom from the madness, some bastard must have clobbered her with something.

And her little midget, too.

*

Edie couldn't believe it had worked. And she said as much. "I'll be buggered backwards with a broomhandle," she said. "It's only gone and bloody worked!"

She left the projectionist's booth and headed down to the foyer, where everything was going tits-up. A lot of the little fuckers had managed to reach the doors, but there were still plenty for her Larry to get a hold of, once he'd finished playing around with Willem Dafoe.

"*Sona si Latine loqueris!*" she cried, concentrating only on the doors at the front of the foyer, through which the little bastards were fleeing. As if by magic—which was, in fact, what it was—the doors all slammed shut. One poor lady was half-in half-out when it happened, and it split her right down the middle. The portion on the inside slid down the glass while the bit of her that was outside blew away in the wind.

"Honk if you know Latin?" said the event organiser. "That's what you just said."

"It worked, though, dinnit?" said the witch, turning to face the whiny little man. He ran away without a further sound. Off to some panic-room, Edie thought, where he would barricade himself in and eat Spam until he died of middle-age.

There was something missing about all this. Edie still couldn't see Larry. "Where's that foolish little piggy of mine?" she said, rolling up invisible sleeves and marching toward the screening of *Larry 3D*.

She barged through the doors, followed the little lights all the way up the ramp, and emerged into the theatre proper, which was now, apart from fifty or so squashed people, completely deserted. She stepped over a couple of heads, tripped on a broken arm, composed herself just before she arrived at the little section they keep for wheelchair users.

At the front of the room, Larry was still going hammer and tongs with Willem Dafoe.

"Put 'im down, son!" she cried. "You don't know where he's been!"

"MA!" Pigface said, still unable to shake the veteran actor from his back. "It's okay, Ma! His willy isn't out!"

Edie shuddered. She really didn't want to get involved in her son's fights—hadn't since Billy Mackem pulled a four-year-old Larry's Y-fronts down at a birthday party many moons ago, and she'd set fire to Billy Mackem's hair in retaliation—but this was going on for far too long. There were kids out there ripe for the killing, and that voodoo hoodoo nonsense wasn't going to keep the doors shut forever.

"Hold 'im still, Larry!" Edie said, rushing toward the front of the theatre. The giant screen now played footage of nothing but the empty cabin; Kathy Bates's legs could be seen twitching at the right of the screen. "Mama's coming!"

Pigface spun around, wheezing and whining as if he'd just climbed out of an elevator with Solange Knowles. Willem Dafoe was stuck to his back like a shell. A crazy shell with crazy eyes and teeth.

"I'm sending you back to Hell, you pig fuck!" Willem said. He bared his teeth and clamped down hard on the top of Pigface's head. Of course, the mask took the brunt of the oversize incisors, but it still must have hurt a bit, for Pigface squealed like the back end of a Christina Aguilera song.

Edie had seen enough. She reached up and grabbed onto Willem Dafoe's legs. "… little… fucking… lunatic! Leave 'im alone!"

"Get offa me!" Willem Dafoe yelled.

"*You* get offa *me*!" Pigface added, bringing his axe up and past his own shoulder in an attempt to catch Willem in the face. And he did. And the axe squeaked like a clown's nose—*har-harr*—and bounced away. And so Pigface said, "Fuck. This axe is nothing but a prop."

"That's right," said Willem, in that tough guy way the hero usually does when he's got one over on the villain. "You brought it with us out of the film. That axe is no more real than you are."

"You don't tell 'im he ain't real!" screeched Edie, still tugging on Willem Dafoe's legs. But it was no use. Willem Dafoe was a lot stronger than he looked. But that was the thing with zany method actors; you should never underestimate them.

It was time for a change of tack. Edie was angry with herself for not thinking of it sooner.

She released Willem Dafoe's legs, and Larry shot off across the room with the little jockey on his back, nibbling at the rubber porcine ears of his mask.

"This is how I die!" Pigface howled. "For the third time! And I haven't even had a chance to kill, yet. Apart from the woman who looked like something that rhymes with Bathy Kates! Ah! Death by Dafoe! Ah!"

Edie pulled the axe from her cloak. This one was very real, and still covered with bits of gore from the projectionist's booth. "Yer'll 'ave to 'old 'im still, son!" she screeched. "I've got a real 'un. This 'un won't go *har-harr*!"

Pigface galloped back toward Edie, slowed down just in time, and spun around as fast as he could. "Quick, Ma!" he said. "I think he's trying to get his willy out!"

But Willem Dafoe didn't have time to get his willy out, for the axe stuck in his back with a meaty thud, and he groaned, exhaled, and slid from Pigface's back like a Crisco-covered cagoule.

The man, the legend, Willem Dafoe was dead. The axe had caught him in that sweet spot just left of the spine, fourth lumbar down.

"What a crazy guy," Edie said, nudging the corpse with her foot. "I thought he'd never let go of yer."

"Ma!" Pigface said, ripping the mask up and over the top of his head to reveal his face.

The face of her son. Her Larry. Her favourite dildo-rinser. He looked just as he had the last time she'd seen him; old, weird, and ugly as sin. He had reached an age where the mask was an improvement. He looked like she imagined Tom Waits's testicles to look.

Still, she pulled him in to a tight hug and tried to ignore the pubic hairs brushing against the side of her face.

"How, Ma?" Larry asked. "How can I be here? Did you do this?"

Edie pulled her head away from her son's (before nature got the better of her and she vomited all down his white apron) and said, "I took a course. I'm a fully-fledged an' paid-up member of the Voodoo Priestess-hood. It's amazin' what'cha can do through the Open University."

Larry stared down at the axe protruding from Willem Dafoe's back. "Is that…"

"I thought yer might need it, what with all these kids runnin' about the place, shittin' themselves."

"You're the best mother I've ever had!" Larry said, and he went to pull Edie into another tight embrace.

"Fuck off, son," she said.

Larry did as she said. He pulled the mask back on and ripped the axe from Willem Dafoe's back. "So there are still plenty of teenagers out there, are there?" He motioned to the aisle leading out of the theatre. "Lots of horny little fuckers? Casual drug-takers? Are there any little fluffy-heads in wheelchairs, because I know a guy over at Crystal Lake who macheted the shit out of one of those, and he reckons it was the best he's ever had?"

"Just go and have some fun, son," said Edie, settling down into an empty chair. Of course, all the chairs were empty now.

Like at a Yoko Ono concert.

"Are you not going to come and watch?" Pigface said.

Exhaling, breathless after her recent scuffle, she said, "I'm too old fer all that massacring malarkey. I'm just going to sit 'ere and watch the end of the film." She motioned to the screen. Kathy Bates's legs were no longer twitching. In fact, not a lot seemed to be happening. It was a bit boring, if Edie was being honest.

"Okay, Ma!" Pigface said. "I'll come get you when I'm done. Enjoy the rest of the… whatever that is." He pointed to the screen. "These kids ain't gonna know what's hit them!"

He *squeeed* excitedly before running down the ramp toward the screen exit, axe raised high.

"That's my boy," said Edie, closing her eyes and yawning. All this voodoo Priestess shit was tiring work. They didn't tell her that when she'd signed up for the course.

Her job complete, she needed to rest.

She was asleep and drooling into her own beard tuft thirty-eight seconds later.

ELEVEN

Jackie Haig sat in the dark for an interminable amount of time, afraid to move in case anyone saw her. Could pigs see in the dark? Was that one of their things? Or was it like when your parents told you to eat your crusts up because it would put hairs on your chest? Complete bollocks.

Jackie Haig's hairy chest had come from HRT, not the end pieces of a sliced white bloomer.

Great, Jackie thought. *Now I'm hungry.*

As if in agreement, her stomach growled, and she did the first thing that came to mind. She shushed it as if it were a recalcitrant child. And then she shushed herself for shushing her stomach. It was a vicious cycle, and one that would get her murdered if she didn't knock it off this instant.

When the chaos erupted in the screening of Larry 3D, she had fled the same as everyone else. At least, everyone except for those poor bastards beneath her feet. Those people weren't doing much fleeing at all. They were part of the décor, now. Smooshed into the Coke-and-ice-cream-stained carpet like so many cockroaches.

Everyone had been rushing for the exits, trying to reach their cars and get away as quickly as possible. But Jackie Haig was no fool. She had seen enough theatre shootings to know that the best thing to do when a killer is on the loose is to hunker down and wait for it all to blow over. Nine times out of ten the asshole with the gun will shoot himself. The ten percent of the time when the shooter hasn't got the balls to do that, the cops give him a hand. It's the way it works, part and parcel of working at a multiplex.

So now here she was, hiding behind the seats in an empty screening of Psycho. Up on the screen, Anthony Perkins was going a little mad—as do we all, according to his character, Norman Bates—and Janet Leigh was about to get all soapy and bloody.

This scene had terrified Jackie as a young lady. It had put her off showers for good (which also might have had something to do with her chest hair) and, thus, she hadn't watched it in years.

But now she was watching it through the space between the headrests in front of her, wondering if it was all over yet. If the loony in the pig mask had been taken down by the cops.

What the hell had happened back there? One minute she had been nose deep in midget, the next people were screaming at the giant pig-man emerging from the screen. Or perhaps they had been screaming at the giant Willem Dafoe emerging from the screen. Either way, it had been the single-most terrifying thing Jackie Haig had ever seen. And she'd once worked security for Roman Polanski.

My phone! Jackie thought, in what would have been a lightbulb moment, if you were allowed to bring lightbulbs into a movie theatre.

She reached into her back pocket and pulled out a Nokia 3210. Granted it wasn't the snazziest of phones, but it was the industry standard for security guards, since you could throw it at a perpetrator, throw it through a window to make good an escape, wear it over your heart as extra protection in case of gunshots, throw it at yourself if the job got too tough, and it would remain intact and in perfect working order.

No bars.

Shit!

She slipped the phone back into her pocket and began crawling along the row. Now, Jackie knew she'd missed the last three Slimming World classes, but the chairs bulging either side of her did her self-esteem no good at all. Also, people had dropped a lot of popcorn as they'd rushed from the screening, and it would be rude not to hoover it all up as she went.

Fortunately, some of it had already been chewed; there wasn't much crunch to it.

As she reached the end of the row, Jackie knew it was time to man-up. Whatever that thing was back there, it was her job to take care of it. She was the security for this event, and she would earn every cent of her seven-dollars-per-hour, or her name was not Jackie William Haig.

She clambered to her feet, took out her pepper spray, and began to descend the steps toward the screen.

The black-and-white shower—in that black-and-white bathroom in that black-and-white creepy-ass motel—was on now, and spraying water all over Marion Crane's beautiful body.

It was a body which would look very different in a few seconds. A lot more holes, that body would have. More gashes than a Kardashian family get-together.

But Jackie Haig didn't have time to watch the scene. She was in the middle of manning up, and manning up meant going back there and taking down that gigantic man-pig.

She was just about to do so when the doors to her left squeaked on their hydraulic hinges.

"Aw, hell no," she muttered, dropping back to her knees and scuttling between Row L and Row K like some bloated beetle—not Ringo Starr.

She could hear the newcomer breathing heavily, even over the sound of water running from a 5.1 Dolby Stereo shower. And then he spoke, and what he said made the hairs on Jackie's chest stand on end.

"I know you're in here," he said. "I always know."

It was all Jackie could do not to scream out loud. The sonofabitch was going to go from row to row, searching the floor for hiding people. He would find her, see her arched back down here amongst the half-empty soda cups, and—

"Oh!" he said. "I guess there's no one here. My mistake. I'll just fuck off, then, shall I?" A slight pause. "I'm going. Because there's clearly no one in this particular screening. Bye."

Jackie couldn't believe her luck. She exhaled, gave it a few seconds, and then backed out of the row. There really was no other way for her to do it. Once out in the aisle, and now laughing hysterically, she got to her feet.

"SQUEEEEE!" said the pig-man. He was right there a few steps away.

"AHHH!" said Jackie. Was it possible to choke on your own heart? In that moment, Jackie thought so. "You tricked me," she said to the bastard in the pig mask. "You said you were leaving, but you *weren't* leaving, *were* you? You're still here."

"I've been known to lie on occasion," said the pig-man. His tongue darted in and out of the mask's mouth slit as he licked at the blade of his bloody axe. It was a disgusting thing to behold; Jackie hadn't been this thoroughly sickened since Fergie pissed herself on stage.

She took a few steps back, up, away from the lunatic. "Who are you?" she said. Suddenly there didn't appear to be any air in the room; every breath was a fight. "What are you going to do to me? I'm security. I'll pepper-spray you!"

She held out the small spray and depressed the button (not by telling it all about how much the UK pound had fallen in the last twelve months). Capsaicin arced out of the nozzle, splashed her attacker square between the snout.

"Take that, you son of a sow!" Jackie said, for it sounded good inside her own head.

For a moment, nothing happened. The pig-man kept on coming, one step, two step, a third, and then the pepper spray must have taken hold, for he said, "Fucking OW!" and slapped a hand to his face. Then he began to splutter and cough uncontrollably. "You… owl… pepper… pig!"

For some reason, Jackie was beset by an image of a little precocious girl-pig in a red dress. Lord knows why, but she imagined the anthropomorphic creature to be a repugnant cunt.

"That's right!" Jackie said, still holding the pepper spray out. "You fuck with theatre security, you're fucking with the wrong people. We got mace, bitch!"

The pig-man stopped choking long enough to say, "You're gonna pay for that. I'm really gonna enjoy cutting you up into tiny pieces."

Jackie depressed the button once again, but this time as the liquid sputtered out the pig-man ducked it and threw himself forwards into Jackie's hefty torso. Jackie grunted as he thumped into her; the pepper spray flew from her hand as she went down, and…

*

…suddenly water. Water everywhere. It was running down her back, running down her front, running between her toes, running between her various downstairs cracks and crevices. Hot water it was, too. The smell of shampoo made Jackie open her eyes.

She was standing in a bathtub. But this wasn't just any old bathtub. It was a black-and-white bathtub. The shower curtain in front of her was monochrome also, as were the tiles on the wall and the water spouting from the showerhead above her.

"What the…"

Her own body was grey, too. Except for the massive black bush between her legs, she was more shades of grey than the shitty book she'd picked up last year at a garage sale.

Psycho…

Turning the water off, and taking a hot-water tap to the rectum, Jackie suddenly realised what was going on here. As crazy as it sounded—and it sounded crazier than Bobcat Goldthwait on helium—she was in the movie.

She was in *Psycho*.

"Aw, hell no!" she said.

That was when she saw the shadow cast upon the shower curtain.

"Hell no!" she reiterated.

Then the curtain was drawn across, and the pig-man was there, only now instead of a filthy and bloody apron he was wearing a flowery little number and what appeared to be a Lucille Ball wig.

Jackie tried to push herself back against the tiles, but it was no use. There was no escape, and she'd already anally ingested a bar of soap and two rubber ducks.

She held out a hand, as if that might help. It didn't. It just ensured the hand was the first thing to be lopped off by the pig-man's axe.

"*Squeee, squeee, squeee, squeee, squeee!*" the pig-man sang as he brought the axe down again and again, thumped it into Jackie body as if she were a tree and he was doing all he could to fell her. "*Squeee, squeee, squeee, squeee, squeee!*"

The first fifteen cuts were the worst.

The sixteenth one took her head off.

After that, and rightly so, she lost count.

TWELVE

"What's going on here?" Wally Perkins asked Ryan Phillipe, CGI Zombie #3021, and Laurence R. Harvey. They had all gathered in the maintenance man's cupboard, for it seemed the safest place to be with that loony witch out there, throwing spells around like a speed-infused Harry Potter. "What did you boys see?"

"I didn't see anything," said Laurence R. Harvey. "I was knocked over by a girl wearing a midget jockey on her back."

"What about you, Phillipe?" Wally turned to the former megastar. "Did you see anything?"

"I saw this little fella get knocked over by a girl wearing a midget jockey," said Ryan Phillipe. "I think my foot's in a mop-bucket. It feels all wet down there."

Wally couldn't believe his luck, and he said as much. "God's got it in for me. I hold this event once a year—that's all, once a year—and now there's some crazy bitch performing necromancy in the foyer, a pig-mask wearing slasher traipsing about the place as if he's the fucking Queen of Zimbabwe, and I'm hiding in a stinking broom cupboard with Ryan shagging Phillipe and the ugly little dwarf from films I'll never watch."

"Hey!" said the ugly little dwarf. "You leave Ryan Phillipe alone. It's not his fault they didn't invite him back for the sequels."

"And you leave the ugly little dwarf alone!" said Ryan Phillipe. "It's not his fault he's a) ugly, b) little, or c) a dwarf."

"I'm not actually a dwarf," said Laurence R. Harvey.

"Really?" said Ryan Phillipe. "What is it, then? Troll?"

"Just a little man," said LRH.

"Goblin?" Ryan Phillipe ventured.

"Sprite, probably," Wally added.

"I'm not a fucking sprite," said LRH. To Ryan Phillipe he said, "At least I was in a sequel, pretty-boy. What was it? *Cruel Intentions 2* too much to take on?"

"I died at the end of the—"

"I don't give a flying fuck!" said LRH. "Can we just concentrate on what we're going to do to get out of this damned place? I've had enough for one convention. We never have this kind of trouble at London Comic Con."

"You're rather quiet," Wally said to CGI Zombie #3021, who was pressed up against the corner so that his pixels didn't accidentally enter anyone. He hated when that happened. "What about a little input?"

"None of this is going to affect me," said CGI Zombie #3021. "I was constructed by the visual effects experts at MPC. I'm not real. You could stick an axe in me for hours and, sure, I'd pretend the axe was doing a good job, but the truth of the matter is, I'm immortal."

"You're a twat," said Wally. He turned back to Ryan Phillipe, who was ringing stale bleach-water out of his slacks. "You're a young man, Phillipe. Why don't you go out there, wrestle the witch to the floor, take the axe from the pig guy, and be the hero of the hour?"

"I'll tell you why," said Ryan Phillipe. "Because there will, at some point down the line, be a follow-up, and you can guarantee I won't be asked to take part in it. *That's* why."

Wally couldn't believe this. They were a bunch of cowards, one and all. "What about you, Harvey?" he said. "If you get us all out of this maintenance cupboard in one piece, I'll throw in free Ben & Jerry's for life. You look like a man who enjoys ice-cream."

"What the hell's *that* supposed to mean?" said LRH. "I don't have to take this shit from you, you know. I can stay at home and be insulted."

"Fuckit!" said Ryan Phillipe. "I've put my other foot in the bucket now."

Wally Perkins sighed. He was one Phillipe-foot-in-a-mop-bucket away from taking his chances out there, with the witch and the pig-man.

*

Pigface fell from the screen, rolled a couple of times before coming to a halt against the front row seats.

What had just happened? He'd been, for some reason, momentarily resplendent in floral housedress and what appeared to be a Michael Ball toupee (though he might have been wrong about the toupee). And the security woman had been standing in a shower, all soapy and hairy and… hairy downstairy.

It made no sense whatsoever, and yet he was willing to play along.

I think you were in a film, said a voice. It was a voice he hadn't heard for a while: that of the mask, which spoke to him on occasion, when the fancy took it.

"I don't think that's possible," said Pigface. He climbed to his feet, picked up his axe, and took a deep breath. That had been some sweet killing. Even in black and white the blood had looked fantastic. Not like that cheap-ass shit they used in Operation Neptune Spear (or the death of Bin Laden, as it was more commonly known).

Take a little look at yourself, suggested the mask. *Go on. I'll bet you're still black-and-white, aren't you?*

Pigface looked down at his body. Even though the theatre was dark, he was still visibly sans colour. "I don't get it," he said. "How's that poss…" He trailed off there, for he remembered that his mother was the brainwave behind this entire resurrection. "It's that Latin thing, isn't it—"

Of course it's the Latin thing, said the mask. Your mother wouldn't know Latin if it jumped up and bit her in the *asinus.*

"She's done something," Pigface said. "She's mucked up the Latin."

You could say that, said the mask. *Another way to put it is that she's a senile old crone whose dildos should be confiscated until further notice.*

Pigface wasn't hearing any of it; the mask had been known to waffle on. "Look, she brought us back, laid on this wonderful spread of orgy-loving teens for us to get our axe into. So what if she messed up the Latin? It's a tough language, like Klingon or Welsh."

Defend her all you like, said the mask. *But you'd better hope that black-and-white comes out soon. You look like something Dirk Bogarde just spit-roasted for his lunch. You look like something from the first five minutes of The Wizard of Oz. You look like that creepy fucking thing from Le Cochon Danseur.*

Pigface took a seat and waited for the B+W effects to dissipate. When he was about the same colour as Elijah Wood (still a bit off, but passable as human in the light of day) he stood up and sighed.

"Let's go kill us some teens," he said.

Or one of those fluffy-heads in a wheelchair, said the mask. *I hear they're easy.*

THIRTEEN

When Freya woke up, it took her a while to figure out where she was, what was happening, and why there was a midget dressed as a murderous doll drooling on the side of her face.

And then it all came flooding back; the chaos, the twenty-foot Pigface, the eighteen-foot Willem Dafoe, leaving Hank right there and then, because it was easier to do it like that than have a drawn-out conversation about it on Monday. It's a well-known fact that the best time to separate with a person is during a traumatic event.

It worked just fine for the parents of Madeleine McCann.

"Hey," Freya whispered. The midget was heavy. Dead weight. To be quite frank, she just wanted the little sonofabitch off her back. It wasn't that she had anything against the little people, per se, but when one's gobbing all over your ear, it's best to politely let them know. "Hey, Chucky? Wake up!" She was whisper-shouting now, which kind of defeated the point.

Chucky, or whatever his name was, smacked his lips together and groaned.

There was nothing else for it but to follow up with a little more cogency. "Oy! Half-pint! Roll off!"

The little person—*I should perhaps ask what they prefer to be called*, Freya thought—snapped awake, and for a moment he too simply stared about the place with a bewildered look upon his face. Some of his bewilderment dripped down onto the bridge of Freya's nose. "What… where… snfgh…"

"We didn't make it out," Freya said as the little person dismounted. "We must have been knocked unconscious. It looks as if everyone left." She motioned to the glass doors in front. The parking lot was empty, save for a 1958 Plymouth Fury in racing-car red, a souped-up Chevy delivery truck, and a sinister-looking 1957 Cadillac. There was also a shitty 1987 Yugo, but the less said about that, the better, for that was Hank's car. "Hank didn't make it," Freya said.

"Hank?" said the little person. He was trying the doors, but they simply wouldn't budge. Freya ushered him aside and gave it a go herself; even she couldn't open them.

"Hank's… my ex," she said, breathless and resigned to the fact that they were trapped in the theatre. "That car over there is his."

When the little person saw the car, he said, "No wonder he's your ex. Even with all those horror movie vehicles out there, that Yugo is the most terrifying."

They tried the door together, as if that might somehow make a difference.

It did not.

"Someone must have locked up," Freya suggested. But why would they do that? Why would anyone shut the place down while there was a twenty-foot serial killer roaming around?

Pigface.

"By the way," said the little person. "My name's Billy. Billy Englund. I'm not a child, but I'm not a midget either. I'm just small." He held out a hand and Freya shook it. It was so tiny; like shaking hands with a baby or Napoleon's cock.

"Pleased to meet you, Billy," said Freya. "I'm Freya. And I didn't for one minute think you were a midget." It was a lie, of course, but she didn't want to offend the guy.

"Step aside, Freya," Billy said, taking several steps backwards. "I'm going to break the glass."

"Maybe you shouldn't—"

"Aaaaaaagggggghhhhhhh!" He shot forwards, a man on a mission, a little bundle of madness that would stop at nothing to get out of the theatre in one piece. When he bounced off the glass a second or two later, landed in an untidy heap on the Cola-stained carpet, Freya felt bad for him.

"Shit!" she said, helping him to his feet. "Are you okay, Billy? You hit that door quite hard." An impression of Billy's face, nose all squashed up and mouth contorted into something like pure rage, would be forever imprinted on that bottom piece of glass. Or at least until someone from the glazing company popped around to change it.

"I'm okay," said Billy, although he didn't look it. He looked like someone who had just slammed face-first into a glass pane at eight mph.

Bandy. He looked bandy.

"It's clear these doors aren't going to open for us, Billy," Freya said. "We need to find another way out of here. There's *got* to be a way."

"I'm sure there are *lots* of ways," Billy said, massaging the egg which had sprouted over his busted eyebrow. "I'm also sure that if we go looking, we'll come across Pigface, and then this place will be turned into an abattoir. I don't know about you, but death by axe is not in my top ten ways to die."

"You have a list of ways you want to die?"

"Not *want* to die. Ways I'd go if I could *choose*, like being sucked to death by Helen Mirren, or being machine-gunned to death by a cheesecake while watching reruns of *Little House on the Prairie.*"

"Where does a cheesecake get a machine-gun from?" Freya asked. And then she remembered that time was of the essence. "Never mind. Look, we can't just stand here coming up with blissful ways to part this world. We've got to find a way out of here. That sonofabitch is going to find us, and he's going to—"

"Show us his willy," Billy said, shuddering.

"I wasn't talking about the giant Dafoe. I think Dafoe's the good guy in all this. I meant Pigface."

"Oh," said Billy.

"Oh indeed," said Freya. She was halfway across the foyer when Billy caught up to her.

"Do you think they'll ever make a film out of this? It'd be pretty meta, don't you think?"

Freya shrugged. "Probably won't be a film," she said, "but there's probably some asshole out there willing to give the novel a shot."

*

Hank Pleasance sat in the filthiest toilet cubicle of all time, shivering, trying to piece together the madness as best he could. There was a psycho killer out there, that much was certain. Not to mention the fact that he'd apparently just been dumped by his girlfriend. He didn't know which one to be more pissed off about.

Everyone had made it to the doors. Well, mostly. Freya and her little jockey hadn't. He'd made sure of that with a cheeky elbow to the back of the head.

How dare she dump me.

But then something had happened. There had been a crush, and several people were knocked backwards, away from the exits.

Hank had been one of those unfortunates.

He'd come to, and at first thought he was dead, for everything was dark and quiet, just like he imagined it would be in the afterlife. Turned out there were three squished bodies pinning him down; his face was buried somewhere in one of the corpse's crotches.

After managing to pull himself out from under the dead kids, he'd limped towards the doors only to find that they were stuck fast. The parking lot was all but deserted. Thankfully, his prize Yugo was still out there.

Across the foyer, it had looked as if Freya and her Chucky companion were dead, had been trampled in the melee, along with the rest of the bodies strewn about the place.

Serves her right for dumping me.

That was when he'd heard a loud *squeee* coming from one of the screens. That was when he'd staggered towards the BOOMSTICKS ONLY toilet. And that was where he had been ever since.

But now everything seemed to be quiet out there. His arse was numb from sitting on the toilet for so long, and his legs were deader than Bill Cosby's comedy career. It took a while, but he managed to get to his feet and stamp out the pins and needles, hissing with pain as he did so.

You can't stay in here all day and all night, he told himself. *It stinks of piss, and I'm pretty sure Laurence R. Harvey filled up the toilets in the cubicles either side of me.* He had to get out of there. Not just the lavatories, but the whole building. If he could just make it to his Yugo… just get the bonnet open… just wait for someone to offer him a jump-cable…

Now that the feeling had returned to his legs and derriere, he felt confident enough to unlock the door. He reached down for the slider and… stopped just as something crashed beyond his cubicle.

Someone had just entered the toilet. Someone with heavy breath and even heavier shoes. There came, with this newcomer, the bitter smell of blood and viscera and, for some odd reason, pineapple shampoo.

Hank had seen plenty of horror movies. He knew what to do. He slowly stepped up onto the toilet bowl, being careful not to slip in.

The person (killer?) who had just come in would check the cubicles by glancing through the lower partition. Upon seeing no feet, the killer would move on, satisfied that there was no one to murder to death here. It was your bread-and-butter standing-on-a-toilet-until-the-killer-fucked-off trick, and Hank was playing it like a champion.

"I know you're in here," a voice growled. It was a horrible voice, as if it had been channelled through one of those joke voice-changers you can pick up at gadget stores. "I've never once fallen for the standing-on-a-toilet-until-the-killer-fucks-off trick. I've been doing this for far too long. Plus, I can smell you in there."

Shit, shit, shit, shit… hang on a jeffing minute! You can smell Laurence R. Harvey, not me!

The next time the voice spoke, it sounded as if it was addressing a third person. Were there two of them? Like in that film with Monica from *F*R*I*E*N*D*S* and the least talented one of the Arquettes?

"Yeah, I know there might not be anyone in there," the voice said. "I'm just saying, there's a good chance there is. I mean, the door's locked, it's clearly **ENGAGED**, which is usually a damn good sign there's a fucking kid in there doing his damnedest not to slip into the toilet bowl." A pause, as if the third person was answering, and then, "Sure, it's possible that this particular toilet is out of order and that the slider's been wiggled across from the outside by a janitor who is wholly too good at his job. I'm not saying I'm one-hundred-percent certain there's a kid in there. But I'm at least eighty-percent, and—"

Another pause. Hank was sweating by now. The pins and needles had returned to haunt him.

"I get where you're coming from," grunted the voice. "Toilets are tricky business. But no, I'm not going to slip my head under the door to see if there's anybody in there. Do you know why? Because that's how you take a size twelve boot to the face, that's why…"

Hank didn't know how much longer he could hold it. His legs were wobbly; it was like standing on two strings of overcooked spaghetti.

"Okay, well, we'll agree to disagree, but I think there's someone in there, and I'm in control here, so if you don't mind…"

Hank couldn't hold it any longer. His right foot twisted inwards, slipped off the rim of the toilet bowl, and splashed down in a pond of piss and cigarette butts and, for some bizarre reason, a signed photograph of Ryan Phillipe.

Shit!

"Told you," said the voice. "*Squeeeeeeeee!*"

The head of the axe came through the door. Wood splintered, slivers of which bombarded Hank's face like a plywood bukkake. He tried to free his foot from the toilet, but three of his five toes had slipped around the U-bend and he just couldn't pull it out.

The axe came through again and again, its wielder squealing with delight with every hit. Hank looked up just in time to see a porcine head push through the freshly-chopped hole.

"Heeeeeeeere's Larry!" the killer said.

"Fuck off, Larry!" Hank said before delivering a swift uppercut to the head. The head wasn't quite right, colour-wise. It was the same colour as Elijah Wood.

The pig head snapped back in slow-motion like in the *Rocky* movies. Hank had never seen anything quite like it. Drool slowly seeped from the mouth-slit of the mask, danced through the air, before splatting against the long mirror opposite. Time sped back up just as gravity returned to normal and the spittle stretched down toward the soap dispensers below.

"That wasn't very nice," said the killer. "You could have had my eye out."

Hank desperately pulled at his leg, with one hand while the other fought to keep the pig's head at a safe distance. Perhaps it wasn't the greatest idea he'd ever head, a fact proved when four fingers and a thumb landed on the cubicle floor below.

Screeching in pain, Hank stared at his now fingerless hand as blood sprayed from the stumps. It was his masturbating hand! Nothing would ever be the same again, whatever happened in the next few minutes.

"Let me guess," said the killer. "That was your wanking hand? I'm good, ain't I? Of course, it's all just a matter of statistics. Ninety percent of the population rub one out with their right. The other ten percent are witches." The axe came through the door and thumped into Hank's shoulder. Beneath him, the porcelain was cracking.

He screamed again as the axe was yanked free.

"On the bright side," said the killer. "You get to go like Elvis. You're welcome."

Hank didn't have time to react as the axe penetrated the cubicle door for the final time and embedded itself in the top of his head. For a while, everything was beautiful. There were flamingos and rainbows and Hank as a child, running about an aquarium screaming Fish! Fish!

But then things metamorphosed, became much darker. Here was Hank nursing a grazed knee; there was Hank being fingered by his Uncle Tommy. Here was Hank lost in the park; there was Hank being made to watch the entire run of *My Mother the Car*. All nightmarish, all events which had shaped him into the young man he was today.

Then there came a *squelch*! And Hank felt his body drop from a great height, slap against cold wet tiles as the blackness came up to meet him halfway.

FOURTEEN

CGI Zombie #3021 stepped slowly out of the maintenance cupboard. Just because it couldn't be butchered like the idiots around him, it didn't mean it couldn't be scared. And it was scared. It said as much.

"I'm digitally shitting myself," it said. And it was. Tiny pixelated turds were falling from its backside and landing on the garish red carpet below, where they sat for a while before disappearing completely.

"Why are you being so careful?" Wally Perkins asked through the crack in the door. "I thought you said you couldn't be killed by this prick?"

"Look," said CGI Zombie #3021. "Those guys over at MPC are really good at their jobs, okay? When they created me, they gave me certain human attributes."

"Well, your certain human attributes are falling all over the carpet," Wally said. "Can you just get a wriggle on? Get out there and see if it's safe for us to make a run for it. And if you see that Pigface character, ask him what it's going to take to make him go away without killing us."

CGI Zombie #3021 nodded. It knew what it had to do. Wally Perkins had instructed it to clear the corridor all the way to the Fire Exits at the rear of the theatre.

They could make good their escape that way, providing that the witch or axe-wielding lunatic weren't standing in their way.

It was about to set off when Wally Perkins' head appeared in the crack of the door once again. "Oh, and if you happen to make it to a phone, I want you to call the police—"

"I can't pick anything up!" CGI Zombie #3021 reminded Wally. "How many times do we have to go through this. I've about as much substance as a fart on the wind. I'm lighter than Lindsay Lohan. I'm about as real as a Big Mac—"

"Alright, go on then. Piss off." And Wally's head was gone again. There came the clicking of a key being turned in a lock.

CGI Zombie #3021 was out there in the hallway all alone. It hadn't been this scared since they'd asked it to stand in for a hungover Darkseeker in *I Am Legend*.

"You can do this," it told itself. "You can't be killed, remember? Nothing can hurt you. You're just a series of 0's and 1's. You're like a Tardigrade or Kirk Douglas. There is no end in store for you." Unless, of course, the servers over at MPC went down. In which case it'd be gone in a jiffy.

It really didn't bear thinking about.

It slowly shuffled along the hallway. The posters on either side of it promised new films from Kristen Stewart and Gilbert Gottfried at some point next summer. CGI Zombie #3021 prayed that the servers over at MPC went down before that.

It reached the foyer, saw the bodies scattered about the place like meat confetti, and turned around. "Fuck this," it said. The trouble was, it couldn't run. It was programmed to act like a zombie at all times.

And we all know zombies don't run.

It began to stagger languidly back towards the hallway. And that was when the toilet door flew open and out stepped Pigface. CGI Zombie #3021 knew it was Pigface because it had seen the posters.

The superannuated slasher was covered with blood and gore, though he looked a little sickly. Pasty, like Elijah Wood. When Pigface saw it standing there, gormless, a zombie in the middle of a theatre foyer, he froze. It was a Mexican standoff between digital and celluloid, pig and zombie.

"What the hell are *you* supposed to be?" Pigface asked. "I really don't get this cosplay thing. I mean, I get that people like to dress up as their favourite characters, but why would anyone bother dressing as a zombie? It's tiresome. And for that, I'm going to have to put you out of your misery, kid."

CGI Zombie #3021 turned slowly around and began shambling slowly across the foyer. "Nope," it said. "Nope, nope, nope…" But there was no way it was going to outrun this maniac.

"I like that, kid," said Pigface, following slowly. "Staying in character, despite the fact you're about to get hacked to death. I like that a lot. They ought to give you the trophy right now. Most Dedicated Cosplayer 2017. That'd look good on your mantelpiece, next to your urn."

Pigface was right beside CGI Zombie #2031 now, his axe mid-swing. There was a moment when it thought Pigface was going to miss, though it was just a moment. The blade took CGI Zombie #2031's head clean off. Its head went one way and its body another. When the viscera had settled, it blinked once or twice and then froze. It allowed its body to twitch erratically for a while, and then that too fell still.

"*Squeeee!*" squealed Pigface.

Play dead, thought CGI Zombie #2031.

And that's just what it did as Pigface moved across the foyer, dancing a little jig and congratulating himself on a joke well told.

*

Ryan Phillipe sat in the corner waiting from his trousers to dry. Wally felt sorry for the guy. How could anyone so pretty be so stupid?

"Did either of you ever see *AntiTrust*?" Ryan Phillipe stood up, flicked the remaining bleach-water from his slacks, and climbed back into them.

"Who was in it?" asked Laurence R. Harvey.

Ryan Phillipe looked offended for a few seconds before speaking. It was an expression he had down to a tee. "*I* was," he finally said.

"Then no," said Laurence R. Harvey. "Let me guess, you weren't in the sequel."

"Can we not go through all that again, please?" Wally said. "We're in a tight space here. The last thing we need is more shit flying about the place."

LRH apologised before stretching his legs. They weren't, as legs went, the longest legs, but they were legs nonetheless, liable to seize up the same as regular legs.

"Do you think that digital doofus is going to make it back here in one piece?" he asked.

Wally sighed. He hoped so. They were relying on CGI Zombie #3021 to get them out of there. If things had somehow gone south, they would have to change their plan. Ryan Phillipe would have to go out there, whether he liked it or not.

Suddenly there came a tapping, as of someone gently rapping, rapping at the maintenance cupboard door.

"Nevermore!" said Ryan Phillipe for absolutely no reason at all.

Wally shushed the ex-actor, reminding him that it could be the witch at the door, or the pig-faced slasher. None of them moved, for fear of being heard. And then came a voice—

"He lopped my bloody head off."

—and Ryan Phillipe, LRH, and Wally breathed a collective sigh of relief.

"That you, CGI Zombie #3210?" asked Wally.

"No," came the reply. "I'm #3021. #3210 was an extra on *The Walking Dead*. Bit of a prick, now that he's made it to the big-time. Lots of women throwing themselves at him. Digitally banged the blue girl from *X-*

Men. Sanctimonious bastard. Anyway, you gonna let me in. Got a bit of a problem."

Wally turned the key in the lock and eased the door open. When CGI Zombie #3021 came in carrying its own head, like something that had just wandered over from Sleepy Hollow, Ryan Phillipe went into hysterics.

"Ah! His head's off!"

Laurence R. Harvey walked two feet across the cupboard—a long way if all you have are baby-steps—and backhanded Ryan Phillipe across the face. "Calm down, man!" he said. "The thing isn't real. Didn't you hear what it said earlier? It can't be killed! For the love of God, man, calm down." He slapped Phillipe again, enjoying the second one more than the first.

Wally re-locked the door and turned to CGI Zombie #3021. "Take it things didn't go well?"

The digital representation of an undead bastard nodded towards its own head (a feat in itself) and said, "Swimmingly. This is a new look for me. I think I might keep it."

"There's no need to be like that," Wally said. "Tell us what happened, but firstly, put your head back on, will you? I don't know whether to talk to your face or the place where your face should be."

Once CGI Zombie #3021 had re-installed its phizzog, it said, "Came at me with a bloody axe, he did. Then did a little jig and fucked off down the hallway."

"Who?" asked Ryan Phillipe. "Who came at you with an axe?" It was by far the best acting Wally had ever seen from the guy, although his accent could have done with a little work, for he sounded somewhat Jamaican in places.

"Pigface," said CGI Zombie #3021. "And I know it's the real Pigface because I've seen the posters."

"It could just be a copycat slasher," Laurence R. Harvey suggested. "Like in the sequel to that film with Monica from *F*R*I*E*N*D*S* and the least talented one of the Arquettes?"

"It was the real Pigface," CGI Zombie #3021 reiterated. "No doubt about it. I could see the evil behind the mask. His eyes, they burn through your soul like wildfires. You can practically smell the malevolence oozing from his pores. I fairly shit myself, make no mistake about it. He took my head off with one swipe of his axe. It took Brad Pitt eight attempts in our movie. Of course, he was probably thinking about how to break it off with Angelina at the time, but still…"

Wally slumped down in a corner. It was the corner in which Manny Cinquetento, the maintenance man, kept his empty whisky bottles. Once the glass stopped rolling around the cramped space, he said, "We're fucked. If that thing out there is the real Pigface—and that witch is his real mother—we might as well just lie down right now and wait to die."

Ryan Phillipe lay down and placed his arms across his chest.

"It was a figure of speech," Wally said.

"I know," said Ryan Phillipe. "I'm just really tired. Didn't get much sleep last night. Kids kept pissing through the zipper of my tent."

Wally despaired. He truly despaired. And he said as much.

"I despair. I truly despair."

As a running joke, it was starting to wear a little thin.

FIFTEEN

Freya and Billy made their way through the maze of carpeted corridors. Cinematic explosions and screams of terror surrounded them (like at a Yoko Ono concert), as movies continued to play, oblivious to what was happening in reality.

"How big is this place?" Billy asked. "It seems like we've been walking for hours, and we've yet to come across anything remotely resembling a Fire Exit."

"Five minutes," Freya said. "We've been walking for five minutes. We took a right at the cardboard cut-out of Bruce Campbell, then went straight on at the replica chainsaw from *Texas Chainsaw Massacre: The Next Generation*, and now we're here." She motioned to the hallway around them.

"I feel like I need to rest," said Billy. "My legs aren't as long as they used to be." Whatever the hell that meant. "Do you need to rest?"

"I just want to get out of here," Freya said. "There's got to be some…" She trailed off, for in the distance she could hear sirens. Lots of sirens. "Well, it's about fucking time!" she said. "All those assholes that made it out, and only now one of them has thought to call the cops."

Billy looked as if he might cry. "We're saved," he said. "They're going to break down the doors and rescue us!"

"I wouldn't count on it," said Pigface. He was standing at the end of the hallway, his axe bloody and dripping with guts. "Nobody is going to save you. I'm going to cut your—"

Neither Freya nor Billy waited to hear what Pigface was going to cut from them. They barged their way into the screen opposite.

*

"—noses off and swap them over so that you look really strange," Pigface said, but the girl and the man-child were already gone.

I don't think they heard that last bit, said the mask. *Shame. It was a good one.*

"It was, wasn't it?" said Pigface. "But if they didn't hear it, at least I can use it again later on someone else."

Well, I mean, you could… if you really wanted to.

"You don't think I should?" Pigface began walking along the hall, towards the doors through which they had escaped.

No, no, you do whatever you want to. I was just thinking, it would be nice to mix things up a little, you know? I heard that last wisecrack, you heard that last wisecrack, let's come up with something new, is all—

"Shhh," Pigface said, for they had arrived at the doors.

What do you mean, 'Shhh'? You're the only person that can hear me. If anyone needs to pipe down, it's you.

"Quiet!" Pigface eased the door open and stared into the darkness. It was noisy in there. Chirpy music was booming out through the speakers. Something about "Dance, Magic, Dance." Pigface had never heard anything quite like it. It was a world away from the banjo ditties his Ma used to play for him to put him to sleep at night—if the moonshine and mallet failed to do the trick.

"Squeeeeee!" Pigface roared into the darkness. "Ready or not, here I come!"

That one sucks, said the mask. *Never say that again.*

*

When Freya and Billy arrived at the back row, they were surprised to find someone hiding there. A man. A man wearing a brown fedora, a filthy green-and-red sweater, and plastic knives for fingers. He was a big guy, and for a moment Freya thought the poor bastard had gone and got himself stuck down there between the seats. When he saw them, he squeaked. Up on the screen, Bowie was trying to seduce the shit out of a teenage girl.

Freya crouched down beside the cowering Krueger; Billy didn't have to. "Be really quiet," she said, placing a finger over her lips. At least one of those gestures was superfluous.

Fat Freddy nodded. Freya could see the fear in the poor guy's eyes, could tell he wanted them to just go away and leave him alone, for their arrival had placed him in danger. Placed them *all* in danger.

Billy tugged at Freya's jacket, and when she turned to see what he wanted, he was pointing down toward the screen.

Pigface stood there, limned by the glittery cock of one of glam-rock's (and every other genre, for that matter) most famous and worshipped exponents. He was sniffing at the air, swinging his axe around willy-nilly, and being generally creepy.

Freya placed a hand on Billy's shoulder: *everything is going to be okay.* That sonofabitch had seen them come in here, but there were two doors either side of the screen, which they could have taken. Pigface didn't know they were cowering right at the back of the room.

How could he?

Now Pigface was dancing along Bowie. It was one of the most surreal things Freya had ever seen in her life (and she'd been to a Yoko Ono… okay, never mind).

"There's no way out of here except past me," Pigface said, taking the steps two at a time, then one back down, then two up, then one down. The bastard was loving this. Every single moment of it.

And, Freya thought, he was right. Unless they clambered over the seats in front, they were trapped.

Up on the screen, Bowie fannied around with three little crystal balls.

"I don't know who this big-haired hermaphrodite is, but he can sure carry a good tune." Pigface swung his axe in time with the music. "I wonder if he'll be on tour anytime soon. Ma would love the shit out of this!"

We're sitting ducks, Freya thought. *He's going to come up here, and he's going to slash us all to pieces, probably dancing while he does it.*

Pigface was up to Row M when Freya stood up. Hiding seemed pointless. They were fucked, either way. Was it not better to go down fighting? Perhaps, as a trio—albeit a rag-tag one—they could overpower the maniac. He was just one man, was he not? Granted, he was a slasher, and therefore took a lot more killing than ordinary men, but still…

"Ah!" Pigface said cheerfully. "There you are! Right at the back, where the boys and girls play with one another in the dark."

Billy peeled himself off the chair next to him and grimaced.

"Come on, you asshole!" Freya said, her voice filled with fury. "We're not running from you. Come and get some!"

"Actually," Fat Freddy said, pushing himself up from the floor and holding his hand up, as if to ask a teacher a question, "I was thinking about running some more."

Pigface squealed with delight. "Ah! A newcomer!" he said. "I'd never have known you were down there if you hadn't made your presence known. Thanks for that."

Fat Freddy said, "Fuck."

With a hellish squeee, Pigface began to rush up the steps toward them. Freya placed Billy behind her and braced for impact.

If I could just take that axe from him, she thought, *there's a good chance we'll get through this.*

Six feet…

Five…

Three…

And then the strangest thing happened, and for as long as Freya lived, she would never be able to explain it.

One minute they were standing there on the very back row of the theatre anticipating the arrival of an axe-wielding, pig-mask-wearing psychopath, the next…

They were all up in the air. Just floating there, as if the atmosphere had been sucked from the room; as if God had decided, for just a moment, that gravity was no longer relevant and that it would be far funnier watching the human race hovering about the place, bumping into clouds and shit.

Pigface looked just as shocked as the rest of them. At least, as shocked as an expressionless mask could look.

Up on the screen, Bowie was tossing some goblin into a bog of eternal stench.

"Erm, Freya?" Billy said. "I'm pretty sure this shouldn't be happening." He had drifted over to the wall and was trying to grab a hold of one of the dim lights hanging there.

"I'm sure there's an explana—"

That was as far as she got before the words were snatched from her throat, and she—and everyone else in the room—were snatched from one world and sucked inexorably into another.

SIXTEEN

Detectives Ricks and Murtow arrived on scene, a convoy of cop cars trailing behind them with their cherries lit and their sirens wailing.

Murtow—for Ricks was suicidal, and therefore not permitted to drive—swerved and veered around the parking lot before hitting the brakes fifty feet from the multiplex entrance. Tyres bit into the concrete, smoke drifted up into the air, and the car finally came to a halt.

Ricks jumped out of the car, did a little roll as he pulled out his handgun, then pushed himself back against the vehicle, panting and ready for war. It was all very dramatic, if you like that sort of thing.

Murtow didn't.

He was too old for this shit.

After instructing the officers that they were to stay back, Murtow walked around to Ricks' side of the car and crouched down beside his reckless partner. "Okay," he said, "let's run through this again. Male, possibly armed with an axe, possibly wearing a pig mask, possibly twenty-foot tall." He sighed. "I'm too old for this shit."

Ricks ran a hand through his mullet and hit himself thrice in the face with the barrel of his handgun before speaking. "Remember that time we took down those South Africans, and I got to shag Patsy Kensit?"

"What's that got to do with anything?" Murtow asked.

"Nothing at all," said Ricks. "I got to shag Patsy Kensit. Just like reminding you."

Murtow turned his attention to the multiplex, upon which hung banners and posters advertising some sort of horror film festival. "Kids," he said, shaking his head. "I'm too old for—"

"Never mind all that now, Murtow. What are we gonna do? We gonna bust in there, shoot us some suspects before giving them a chance to explain themselves, then involve ourselves in a massive car chase, one of those ones where I start off running and you have to pick me up after, and then I end up jumping off a bridge and landing in a truck filled with marshmallows, or some other soft shit, and then the bad guys get away— for now—because it wouldn't be very exciting if we brought them to justice straight away? Is that the plan?"

"Actually," said Murtow, "I thought I'd start off by shouting through this loudhailer thingamajig." He held up the loudhailer thingamajig. "See if I can get the twenty-foot pig to give himself up."

"I'm never going to shag Patsy Kensit again, am I?" Ricks said.

Murtow patted his partner on the shoulder. "There'll be others," he said. "Now, can I have a bit of quiet while I try to negotiate with the bad guys?" He stood up; his back cracked like he was wearing a suit knitted from bubble-wrap. He fumbled with the loudhailer thingamajig for a couple of seconds before figuring out how to switch it on. He cleared his throat before beginning.

"This is the Detective Murtow of the Badonkadonk Police Department. We've got the whole place surrounded. Come out with your trotters up or we will open fire. Many of us will miss the whole building, more than two thirds of us will accidentally shoot a colleague, but a couple of lucky shots might get through. You have been warned. This is your last chance. I'm too old for this shit."

Ricks nodded and turned his attention to the multiplex entrance. "You think he'll give himself up?"

"I hope so," Murtow said. "Tish is doing lamb casserole for dinner. She'll bust my ass if I'm not back to enjoy it."

"Am I invited?" Ricks asked.

"Do you promise not to try to molest my fifteen-year-old daughter again?"

Ricks nodded.

"And no stabbing yourself in the face with the steak knives?"

Ricks nodded again.

"I'm too old for this shit," said Murtow.

*

One eye flickered open, and then the other. Willem Dafoe didn't know where he was, or what was going on. All he knew was that he had a real pain in the back, and that he was lying in a pool of blood (his own?), which was never a good sign.

Someone was shouting something. It sounded fuzzy, as if the words were being filtered through a loudhailer thingamajig. He had starred in plenty of movies in which his characters had to use loudhailer thingamajigs. Willem Dafoe was a lot smarter than he looked, which was fortunate.

He got to his feet, skidded for a moment on the blood puddle—like some sort of drunken Pingu—then managed to steady himself.

A snort to his right startled him. He turned, saw the old witch asleep on the front row, and it all came flooding back. The battle with Pigface, the crone pulling at his legs, the sudden death by axe, it all played out in his head. It would, Dafoe thought, make a great movie someday.

Or perhaps a novel?

Of Pigface or the axe there was no sign. Willem Dafoe feared the worst. If that asshole had got out, there could be hundreds of kids dead already.

"Not on my watch," grunted Willem Dafoe. He stumble-slipped his way across the floor, coming to a halt in front of the snoozing crone. He slapped her once around the face, and then a second time more forcefully. When her rheumy eyes snapped open and her toothless mouth fell open, he said, "Where is he?"

The witch blinked the sleep away. "You're… you're dead!" she gasped. "I put an axe in yer back!"

"Oh, is that what that agonising pain is?" Willem Dafoe shrugged. "You can't kill Willem Dafoe, bitch."

"I thought that was Chuck Norris," she said.

Dafoe frowned. "Yeah, well, it *might* be… but Willem Dafoe's tough, *too*. Now tell me where that evil bastard son of yours is, or so help me God I'm going to rip out your intestines and string you up by them."

"You an' whose army?" cackled the crone. "Look at'cher. You look like you ain't slept fer weeks. You ain't got the balls to 'urt an old lady."

"I blew up Aunt May," Dafoe said. "Lady, you have no idea what I'm capable of." He wrapped his hands around her throat and gave a gentle squeeze. That was all it took. The crone began to choke and talk at the same time.

"I don' know where he is!" she spluttered. "He was 'ere, an' then he wasn't. Left 'im to 'is own devices, I did." Her face had reddened and blue veins stood out on her cheeks and forehead. She looked a lot like a road-map of Nevada, only with more hair.

Willem Dafoe released her. The old bitch was right. He couldn't kill her, no more than he could act in a romantic comedy or keep his willy in his trousers.

"I'm going to kill him," Dafoe said. "You know that, don't you?"

The old lady shrugged, indifferent. "I'll jus' bring 'im back again," she said. "Reckon it gets easier the more you do it."

"You're sick!" Dafoe said.

"Thanks," she replied.

Willem Dafoe punched her once to the temple, put her straight to sleep. As she began to snore once again, he moved quietly through the theatre, down the carpeted ramp, and out through the doors, being careful not to let them slam shut behind him as he went.

*

"Is it time for the tear-gas?" Ricks asked. "Doesn't look like our perp's going to cooperate. Maybe I should take off my shirt, you know? Go on in there alone, have a bit of a scuffle, get knocked unconscious, wake up over a bucket of water with a five-foot Japanese guy shocking the shit out of me with sponges?"

"I'll try the loudhailer again," said Murtow.

SEVENTEEN

"I don't think we're in Kansas anymore," Billy said, motioning to the myriad strange creatures dancing all around them. Some of them wore tiny brass helmets, others were covered from ugly head to hobbit foot in hair. It was just like being at a Yoko Ono concert (last one, I promise).

"We're not," Todd said. He'd told them his name a few seconds before this chapter began, but you weren't there, so you weren't to know. "I think… I think we're in *Labyrinth*."

"That's not possible, Todd," Freya said, peeling an eyeball-covered plant away from her ankle. But even she had to admit the whole scene looked familiar. There were walls on all sides of them, or so it seemed. She had seen the movie enough times to know that there was probably a gap there somewhere, concealed, a way through to the Goblin King's castle. On the floor, someone had marked the way with lipstick arrows. "This isn't right," she said. "I mean, it can't be real!"

Billy was having a conversation with one of the goblins.

"Billy!" Freya said. "Don't talk to it. You don't know what it is, or what it's capable of."

Seemingly offended, the goblin scuttled away, disappearing into a small hole at the base of one of the walls.

"It was telling me where it got its clothes from," Billy said, pulling at the straps of his Good Guys dungarees. "Did you know they've got a GAP here?"

"I did not know that," Freya said. "But it wouldn't surprise me."

They walked for a while, first one way and then the other. If there *was* a secret passageway, it was well concealed. "If this is *Labyrinth*," Todd said, more than a little out of breath and sweating like Gary Glitter's paperboy, "and we have, somehow, been sucked into the movie, then where the hell did Pigface go? Shouldn't he be here, too? He came through with us."

Freya nodded. Todd was right. They had all been floating around that theatre like turds in a bathtub, Pigface included. "He's here, somewhere," she said, suddenly feeling very nervous. "We have to keep our wits about us. Stick together, and whatever you do, don't talk to any of the flora or fauna."

"*Them's my jewels!*" came a whiny voice.

For fuck's sake, Freya thought. *This is ridiculous.*

*

Willem Dafoe, now armed with an ice-cream scoop he'd managed to procure from the concessions stand, cautiously walked across the foyer. Beyond the glass doors, two stereotypical eighties cops were trying to force entry. The one with the mullet was smashing his face against the glass repeatedly in an effort to break it. The black cop was shaking his head and repeating something over and over. Dafoe tried to read the cop's lips.

I'm… too… gold… for… this… sheet…

It didn't make much sense to Dafoe, but he had faith in the law.

He made his way to the glass doors. When the cops saw his approach, they both grinned and pointed, as if they were familiar with him.

"Yes," Dafoe said. "I am Willem Dafoe, one of the finest actors of our generation, second only to all other actors. Won't it open?"

The mulleted cop shook his head and, as if to prove it, slammed his face against the glass one more time. A tooth fell from the cop's mouth, but he didn't seem to care, simply shrugged: *see?*

"I think it's some kind of magic," Dafoe said. "There's a witch woman in here with us. I think she's cast a spell over the entire theatre."

The cops nodded as if they understood. The black cop took out his shield and pressed it against the glass. The mulleted one did the same.

"Ricks and Murtow, huh?" Dafoe said, examining the badges. "Well, Ricks and Murtow, I'm your man on the inside. For want of a better description, I'm your John McClane. However, I refuse to take my shoes off, and I look shit in a white vest. But I will resolve this little mutual problem of ours or my name's not Willem Dafoe. And it is."

Murtow gave him a thumbs-up; Ricks took a run-up and bounced off the glass.

"Okay, I'm going to find this sonofabitch and kill him," Dafoe told Murtow. It seemed pointless trying to talk to the other one. "You boys keep trying."

He turned and walked back across the foyer, stepping over mangled bodies and dropped nachos.

Where are you, you piggy motherfucker?

*

Marcia Hodder had never seen the inside of a projectionist's booth before. They were a lot smaller than she imagined. Very cramped. Not great if you suffer from claustrophobia. Or flatulence.

"Do you think we'll be safe in here?" Aretha said, nervously looking about the place. "There's no way to lock this door and—"

"If we just keep our voices down," Marcia said, "there's no reason for anyone to come through that door. We're out of the way here. Down there, we won't last an hour. That asshole's picking us off one by one. Neither of us are virgins; we don't have the necessary attributes of a final girl. We'd be fucked if he found us."

Aretha walked up to the viewing pane, stared down at the screen and the film playing upon it. "Is that David Bowie?"

"*Labyrinth*," Marcia said, nodding. "Used to watch it a lot when we were kids. Can't watch it nowadays without focussing directly on Bowie's magnificent bulge. It's strange how you don't notice things like that when you're an eight-year-old girl, but as soon as you turn thirteen it's like BAM. Right there in your face. A massive cock."

"I can't say I've ever noticed it," said Aretha. "I always thought of Bowie as dickless. Smooth down there, you know? Not like Willem Dafoe—"

"Did someone say my name?"

The girls turned, their faces contorted with terror as they stared into the darkness. Had the killer found them? Were they now sharing a tiny room with Pigface? If so, there was no way out. They would die here, in this muggy box.

But when the man stepped out of the shadows—all cinematic it was, too, like something out of a Nicolas Winding Refn movie—and smiled those rows upon rows of tombstone teeth, the girls relaxed.

"Willem *Dafoe*?" said Aretha. She sighed with relief. "Oh, man, I thought you were dead. The last time we saw you, you were fighting with Pigface."

"You were also three times bigger than you are now," Marcia said. "What the hell's going on?"

Dafoe told them everything that he knew. He told them about the crone, about how he'd taken an axe to the back and survived (because you can't kill Willem Dafoe).

"I thought that was Chuck Norris?" Aretha said.

"Yeah, well, Willem Dafoe's tough too," Dafoe said. "In fact, I once challenged Norris to a duel. And guess what? Old ginger-bollocks didn't show."

Marcia didn't believe that for one second, but she still felt a lot safer having Willem Dafoe around. He reminded her a lot of her own father, inasmuch as they both looked like they'd had fireworks go off in their face.

Dafoe went on. He told them about the two detectives out front and the army of squad cars on the parking lot. He told them that they looked about as efficient as a grave robber in a crematorium.

"But they're cops, though," Aretha said, sounding somewhat hopeful. "They'll get us out of here, won't they? They'll get the bad guy. They *always* get the bad guy… eventually."

"Try telling that to the victims of D.B. Cooper," Dafoe said. "They still haven't caught the McCanns, and those evil bastards are right there, waiting to be arrested."

Marcia wasn't sure she liked Willem Dafoe. There was something about him, something not quite right. Was this the man that was going to save the day. Was he their John McClane? She looked down at his feet, saw that he was still wearing shoes, and sighed.

Willem Dafoe went on, trying to comfort Aretha, all the while moving around the tight space searching for anything that could be used as a weapon. Anything was better, Marcia thought, than the ice-cream scoop he was currently armed with.

"Hang on a second," Dafoe said, suddenly. He had come to a stop in front of the viewing pane, and was staring out at the screen. "I don't remember this scene in *Labyrinth*. I mean, I don't remember much about it, other than Bowie's lady-boner, but I don't think I've ever seen this bit before. Is this some sort of Director's Cut?"

"What are you talking about?" Marcia walked across the tiny booth and glanced out through the pane.

On the screen, a girl—flanked by a fat Freddy Krueger and a midget Good Guy doll, like the world's shittest *The Wizard of Oz* reboot—walked through a concrete maze.

"Hey," said Aretha. They were all standing at the viewing pane now. "I recognise that little guy. I saw him earlier being eaten by the security lady. And I saw that chubby Freddy in line. I'm pretty sure that girl was here, too, with a guy. Yeah, I saw them pull up in a piece-of-shit Yugo. All three of them were here at the con. And now—"

"And now they're in *Labyrinth*," Marcia finished. "Sure, why not?" Willem Dafoe was standing just two inches to her right. Of *course* this was possible. Anything was possible in this fucked-up version of reality they were currently trying to swim through.

"They've been sucked into the movie," Willem Dafoe said. "Just like we were spat out of ours. That witch sure has cocked up the physics in this multiplex."

"How do we get them back out?" Marcia asked. "We can't just leave them in there? Bowie will be all over that poor girl like a hobo on a ham sandwich."

Dafoe shrugged. "We could just stop the movie," he said, motioning to the film running through the projector.

"Might kill them," Marcia said, shaking her head. "No, there has to be another way."

They stood there, silently watching this new strange movie play out on the screen, trying to figure it out. It turned out none of them had a fucking clue.

*

They arrived at a central square, where the walls fell away and trees and shrubs reached up toward the brown-orange sky like monoliths. The little jewel-goblin who looked like a compressed version of Keith Richards had been following them closely, no doubt trying to work out if they were carrying anything of value—the little shit. Freya fought the urge to tell him to fuck off; this was supposed to be a kid's movie, after all, despite its obvious wrongness on so many levels.

There was still no sign of Pigface, which was a good thing. However, there was still no sign of an exit, a way back to reality, which was not so great.

"I always imagined it would be more fun," Billy said, out of nowhere.

"What?" Freya's feet were killing her, and she was gasping for a cup of coffee. They had passed the GAP store a few miles back, but there was no sign of a bloody Starbucks.

"Being in a movie," Billy said. "I always thought it would be exciting, you know? But it's really *not*. It's just a lot of walking around, trying to look pretty for the cameras which you can't see and waiting for something to happen."

"I supposed it depends what film you're in," Todd said. "This is a big landscape, lots of space between here and Jareth's castle. I'll bet it's all happening up there. I'll bet Bowie's doing his thing, and the goblins are all having a party, and Jennifer Connelly will be all woozy from the peach-roofie she just ate. We're just in the wrong part of the film, that's all."

Freya didn't know what was worse; the fact that they were down here, miles away from the Goblin King's castle with a psychopathic pig-faced killer, or that there was a poor girl up there about to be date-raped while a bunch of Henson puppets egged on their honey-voiced overlord.

"Who the hell are you?" a voice suddenly said.

Freya, Billy, and Todd all turned at the same time. Standing there, looking just fabulous in his frilly white shirt, skin-tight trousers, and big-collared jacket stood Jareth the Goblin King, or as he was better known in real-life, David Bowie. Freya's eyes were inexorably drawn to his crotch. *It's not your fault,* she told herself. *It's a subliminal thing, you don't have a choice. No one has a choice!*

None of them spoke.

"I asked you a question. Who the bloody hell are you, and what the fuck are you doing in my Labyrinth?" He tapped his toes; Freya feared he was about to break out in song. She answered quickly, hoping to stifle it before it even started.

"We're looking for a way out," she said. "We're trapped here, you see. Stuck in your Labyrinth. We're not from this world."

"I can see that," said Bowie. "You're from the world's shittest *The Wizard of Oz* reboot, and you should piss off back there before I lose my temper." He turned into an owl momentarily, then changed back. "Sorry about that. Still can't get the hang of it. It comes on quickly, like a sneeze. It's a fucking nuisance."

"Look, we're not the only ones here," Billy said. "There's—"

"How did you get out of the castle?" Bowie said. "And what are you doing out of costume?"

"I'm not one of your goblins," Billy said.

"Then what *are* you? Do you want a job? I need someone to guard the gates to the city. Do you have a driving license? Have you ever used a cleaner? It's like this big pedal thingamajig with a corkscrew on the front—"

"I know what it is," Billy said. "Look, will you just help us. We just want to get back to reality. This place is all fine and dandy, but we don't know what's going to happen once the titles roll. We might die, or we might just start back at the beginning again. Fuck knows. You're David Bowie. If anyone can help us it's you."

Bowie began to think. He said as much. "I'm having a little ponder." It was during said ponder that, somewhere close by, there came a terrifying *squeee*. So terrifying was this *squeee* that Bowie accidentally turned into an owl again. When he returned to human form, he said, "What, in the name of all that is good and pure, was that?"

Freya's heart began to race.

"He's here!" Todd said, turning this way and that.

Bowie was having none of it. "Another one of your lot, is it? Fucking about in my Labyrinth? I've just about had enough of this. Hoggle, hold me back."

The little jewel-goblin rushed across the square, placed both hands on Bowie's crotch, and strained to hold him back. "Them's my jewels!" it said.

Just then, Pigface stepped into the square. He looked tired, breathless, and had picked up a limp from somewhere. "Finally!" he said. "I've been walking around this fucking place for ages. Almost got raped by a bunch of red things that kept taking their heads off and launching them at me."

Bowie pushed Hoggle aside; the jewel-goblin somersaulted, did a little roll, and landed head-first in an animatronic bush. "Now, hang on a minute," he said. "Who are you? You shouldn't be here! Put the axe down, will you? This is a kid's film."

Pigface, doubled over and panting like an excited Labrador, held out a hand. "Give me a second," he said. "Got a stitch in my side. Seriously, have you ever thought about moving somewhere with a smaller garden?"

Freya rushed across the clearing, snapped a branch off a tall tree—the tree went "Ow." Of *course* it did—and turned to face their enemy.

After a few seconds, and many wheezy breaths, Pigface straightened up. "Whew. Okay, where was I?" He looked at Bowie. "Hey, you're the ponce with the nice voice," he said. "Don't suppose you've got any concert tickets going cheap? My ma would love you."

Bowie smiled, seemingly flustered by Pigface's praise. "Actually," he said, "I don't do live shows any longer on account of, well, let's just say 2016 was a bad year for me. I've got some signed pictures back at the castle, though, if your ma's interested?"

"I'll leave it, thanks," Pigface said. "And also, I'm going to have to kill you all now, starting with you!"

It all happened so fast, Freya didn't have time to react. One minute the axe was in Pigface's hand, the next it was somersaulting through the air, and then it was stuck in Todd's chest. It hit him with so much force that he staggered backwards, fell over Hoggle's still-kicking legs, and landed on his back in the grass. As he landed, he instinctively tried to pull it free, but the replica Freddy glove he wore prevented him from getting any purchase.

Perhaps it was for the best.

He exhaled his last breath, choked on a mouthful of blood, and fell still.

Bowie's mouth fell open. "Seriously?" he said. "I have never seen anything so inherently evil in my entire life, and I've been to a Yoko Ono concert."

Pigface said, "Squeee," rushed across the square and pulled the axe from Todd's motionless body. Blood geysered out, painted the front of his filthy apron with fresh crimson. "One down," he said. "Two to go, and I'll take the pretty-boy with the big hair as bonus points."

Hoggle pulled himself free of the shrub and ran off, screaming, "I'm moving to the bog of eternal stench!" at the top of his annoying little voice.

"Now just hold on one minute," Bowie said. "This is your last chance. Either leave this place right now, or I won't be responsible for what happens to you."

Pigface laughed. Snorted. *Squeeed.* Did a little tap-dance. And said, "What happens to *me?* Are you going to *sing* me to death? You going to attack me with hairspray?" He turned to Freya and said, "Looks like you've got yourself a bodyguard here. Just a little tip for you. Don't eat his peaches. I saw a couple of goblins earlier injecting them with Rohypnol."

"Right, that's it!" Bowie said. He unbuttoned his jacket, pulled his skin-tights down (which took wholly longer than it should have) to reveal a small cannon, right there embedded in his crotch where a penis should be. "Weren't expecting that, were you?" he said, seemingly pleased with his man-mortar.

Freya stared down at the thing. It was truly remarkable, a thing to behold—and yet never hold. "Let's just hope it doesn't fire blanks."

David Bowie winked at Freya. "I'm Bowie," he said. "Bowie doesn't fire blanks."

"I thought that was Chuck Norris?" Billy said, not quite sure why he'd spoken at all.

Pigface squealed, rushed headlong toward David Bowie. With a quick flick of the hips, Bowie loaded his cock-cannon.

What happened next would forever stick in Freya's mind, for it wasn't every day you saw a tiny cannonball—no larger than a Hungry, Hungry Hippos marble—shoot through the air and slap a man in a pig-mask right upside the snout.

It must have come sharp, for Pigface said, "Jesus Christ!" and whirled away, moaning in pain. "What the fuck was that? You could have someone's eye out with one of those, you inconsiderate glam bastard!"

But Bowie wasn't done yet. He jerked his hips from side to side, firing again and again, pelting Pigface with round after round. Pigface tried to dodge the tiny cannonballs, but there were just too many of them. It was like dodging raindrops; you were better off just standing still.

"Freya!" Billy cried. "Look!"

Freya turned away from the battle, saw what Billy was pointing at, and said, "Well, that's odd."

And it was odd. Very odd indeed.

A strange vortex had appeared at the edge of the square, just beyond a row of bushes. Within the vortex—

which swirled like water draining away down a plughole—Freya could make out theatre seats, plush and red. She could make out the central aisle and the lights running all the way along it. And she could make out three people standing there in the aisle. They were distorted by the strange ethereal whirlpool, but she could see that two of them were girls, and the third was—

"Is that Willem Dafoe?" Billy said, a slight frown playing about his features.

Freya sighed. "Come on," she said. "That's our door back to reality." She grabbed the little guy by the hand and tugged him toward the vortex.

"Wait!" Bowie shouted after them. "I'm out of ammo!"

Freya, so close to the vortex and subsequently escaping the Labyrinth, turned to find Bowie—the Goblin King, Jareth, Ziggy Stardust—standing there, hands on hips and trousers around his ankles. He looked so vulnerable, so exposed, that Freya felt truly sorry for him.

"I'm sorry," she said. Pigface was rubbing at his wounds across the square, but ultimately he would survive.

"Charming," said Bowie. "In that case, there's a young girl at the castle about to wake up. Time for another peach, methinks." And with that, he transmogrified into an owl once again and took to the sepia-imbued skies.

Pigface growled.

Freya turned and, with Billy firmly affixed to her side like a novelty colostomy bag, leapt into the swirling vortex.

EIGHTEEN

The screen bulged momentarily as an impossibly bright light filled the theatre. Willem Dafoe grabbed the girls by their hands and pulled them away from the screen. It seemed the right thing to do.

"Hold tight!" Dafoe said as a deafening howl emerged from the speakers all around them. "They're coming through!"

The screen bulged until it began to tear, first at the top and bottom, and then the sides. The howl grew louder and the light grew brighter. Willem Dafoe wondered if he'd ever get the chance to expose himself again.

Just when he thought the heavy white vinyl couldn't stretch anymore, it did, only now there were limbs protruding from it. Large limbs, three times the size of regular arms and legs.

Dafoe took an extra step back, just in case.

The girl and her little friend fell out of the screen and crashed down onto the theatre floor, crushing the first two rows entirely with their prodigiousness and buckling the seats in the rows beyond. No sooner had the come through than they started to shrink down.

Up on the screen, Pigface was swinging his axe at—and missing—the whitest owl Dafoe had ever seen. He came close with his axe a few times, but Dafoe figured the owl was just taking the piss.

"Are you okay?" Aretha said, rushing down the steps to help the little guy to his feet. Dafoe did the same with the new girl, who had finally returned to her normal size. At least, Dafoe *figured* it was her normal size. For all he knew, she used to be a six-foot-fiver and had now been handed the shitty end of the stick.

This new girl was a lot tougher than the two he'd met up in the projectionist's booth, and as Dafoe eased her to her feet, she said, "… fuck offa me!" She didn't need any assistance, this one. Dafoe made a mental note and took a step back.

"We saw the whole thing," the one called Marcia said, motioning to the massive screen in front of them. "You were really in there? In the movie? In Labyrinth?"

The new girl wiped the sweat from her forehead, saw the ice-cream scoop in Willem Dafoe's hand, and said, "What you going to do with that, Mr Whippy, serve us a sorbet?"

"It's all I could find," Dafoe said. "You did good in there, kiddo. We thought you were dead, for sure. Happy that you proved us wrong." He handed Aretha a crumpled dollar bill. "She had you down to escape. Guess I underestimated you."

"I don't want to see your willy, Dafoe," the new girl said. "So don't even think about it."

"I wasn't thinking anything of the sort," Willem Dafoe said, pushing the thought from his mind. "I'm just glad you're safe, is all."

"Yeah, no thanks to you!" the little guy said. His name was Billy Englund, apparently, and he wasn't a midget; just a short fella. Everything was in proportion. Except, Dafoe thought, Billy's ears were a little off-centre, like a two-handled trophy crafted by a man working his two weeks' notice.

"We didn't know what to do," said Aretha. "Believe it or not, it's the first time we've ever dealt with interdimensional travel. We thought pulling the plug might leave you stranded in there."

The new girl, Freya her name was, nodded. "Good point," she said. "But…" She pointed up at the screen, to where Pigface was battling a horde of Jim Henson goblins. They were swarming all over him, trying to grapple him to the ground. "We could do that right now, couldn't we? Pull the plug? Strand that fucker in the Labyrinth?"

Dafoe nodded. "In theory," he said. "And it is just a theory. It might do nothing."

"We have to try something," Marcia said. Tears were rolling down her face, smudging her make-up. She looked like she'd just returned from the grave to enact vengeance upon the people who'd put her there.

Dafoe turned his attention to the screen. He froze. "Ah, erm, I don't think we've got time to make it back to the projection room."

Everyone glanced up, saw that Pigface had hacked at least a dozen goblins to pieces and was now urinating upon their dismembered bodies, squeeeing as he did so. Then he looked up—seemed to look directly at them watching him—and tucked himself away.

He started running toward the screen.

"GO!" Dafoe said.

Marcia, Aretha, Freya, Billy, and Dafoe ran down the carpeted ramp. Behind them, the theatre was once again filled with a blinding light and a thunderous roar.

*

Ricks and Murtow were sitting in their car, eating doughnuts and playing Rock, Paper, Scissors, when the captain arrived on scene. They heard him before they saw him, which was usually how they knew he was in the vicinity. Captain Willis was your typical abrasive asshole; he had very little respect for the detectives and officers beneath him, and even less respect for the majors and colonels above him. He was what most people would refer to as an alabaster cocksponge.

"Shit, Murtow!" Ricks said, stuffing the last of his doughnut into his mouth. "It's the alabaster cocksponge."

They climbed out of the car and waited for Willis to finish reducing a dozen or so officers to tears. When he was done, he made his was across the parking lot toward them.

"What in the name of Donald Trump's filthy jockstrap is going on here?" Willis said. A little fleck of spittle landed on Murtow's lip. Murtow chose to ignore it. He ignored it so well that, after a few seconds, he forgot it was there at all.

"Some kind of magic, Captain," Ricks said, motioning to the multiplex doors.

"Magic?" Willis sounded dubious. "You expect me to believe that what is going on down here is all because of magic? Are you shitting me?"

Ricks shrugged; Murtow took over speaking duties.

"He's telling the truth, Captain. We have reason to believe there's a witch in there. We've got reports from at least fifty kids who saw the whole thing go down. A twenty-foot pig-man came through the screen, along with an eighteen-foot Willem Dafoe, and we're trying to get in there, but there's—"

"Whoa, whoa, hold on just a fucking minute, Detective. What did you just say?"

"We're trying to get in there—"

"Before that, you Danny Glover-looking motherfucker! You said something about an eighteen-foot Willem Dafoe. As in Platoon? As in Antichrist? As in the guy who can't keep it in his fucking pants?"

"The very same," said Ricks. "Although, when we saw him not too long ago, we were pleased to discover he was nicely tucked away. Couldn't even see the tip."

"Are you two on drugs?" Willis said. "Is that what this is? You've been at the confiscated lockers again, and now you're having some sort of synchronised hallucination?"

Ricks and Murtow shook their heads. Ricks pushed a small pouch of white powder deeper into his pocket.

"Once I get in there," Ricks said, "I'm going to go full-on Lethal Weapon. I'm going to fight Gary Busey on the front lawn, in the rain, and when you guys come in to rescue me I'm gonna say, 'Nooooooo,' and you'll all back down and let me get on with it, because that's what I do best, Captain."

Willis frowned. Deciding he would get more sense out of Murtow, he said, "I want this thing resolved within an hour, do you hear me?"

Murtow nodded.

"An hour, Murtow, or I'll have both your badges. I'll turn them into fridge-magnets, and then I'll buy a new fridge and let them go with the old one. Then, in a few months' time, you'll be out walking, and you'll walk past an old refrigerator store. You'll peer in, and… what's that, right there on the side of that refurbished fridge? Oh, it's your badges! And you'll cry, because you'll realise that you could have avoided all that if only you'd resolved the fucking issue within an hour. You hear me?"

Murtow nodded.

Ricks licked sugar from his lips.

"Get the fuck out of my face, the both of you." Willis turned and marched past the sobbing officers, back to his vehicle.

"Asshole," Ricks muttered. "You know, one of these days I'm gonna break into that guy's house without a warrant, and then I'm going to shoot him in the leg. He'll fall into his swimming pool, only the plastic cover is still on it, see? And he'll drown in there, wrapped in his own pool cover. Asshole. Oh, by the way, you've got a fleck of spit on your lip."

*

"There are cops out here!" Wally Perkins said as they arrived in the foyer. "They're just standing around. Some of them… it looks like some of them are *crying*?"

"Never a good sign," said CGI Zombie #2031.

They had decided to leave the safety of the maintenance cupboard behind, under the proviso that they all stayed together and had each other's backs. They had paired up (Wally with the digital zombie and Ryan Phillipe with Laurence R. Harvey) in an effort to make it out of the multiplex alive. Wally still had his doubts, but seeing the cops right there, just a few hundred feet away on the parking lot, gave him hope.

"Try to get their attention," said Ryan Phillipe. "Maybe they think we're all dead in here. I mean, it's not as if we've got a man on the inside, is it? A John McClane type."

Laurence R. Harvey had removed his shoes and shirt. Beneath his shirt he sported an already-filthy white vest. He looked like a prize pleb. "What?" he said as they all turned to face him. "I'm just warm, is all. Plus, my shoes are rubbing me. Wish I'd never used my sock to wipe my arse now."

Wally hammered on the door, hoping to attract the attention of the milling officers. A pair of eighties detectives were sitting on the bonnet of a car, staring toward the multiplex and talking. When they saw him, they climbed down and began walking over.

"Oh, good," Wally said. He wanted to know what was being done to get them out of the building. Pity these two didn't look as if they would know much about anything. *Scratch that,* Wally thought. *The white one certainly knows a thing or two about out-of-date hairstyles.*

"Is that a mullet?" said Ryan Phillipe. "Cool!"

"Nope," said Wally. "Not now, not ever. Now shush. Adults are about to start talking."

The eighties cops stopped just short of the doors. The black one, Wally saw, had a fleck of spittle on his lip. *Should I tell him?* Wally thought. *It was one of those things. It's cool to tell someone you know that they have spit on their lip, but a complete stranger…?* He decided not to. Besides, there were more important matters to deal with.

"We're trapped in here," Wally said, unsure whether he should be raising his voice or keeping it to a whisper. As a result, his voice went up and down like an a-cappella fart.

"We know that," said the mulleted one. "But you might want to keep it down a bit. There's a slasher in there with you. And a witch."

Wally nodded. "Yes, we're fully aware of that. Is there any chance of you getting us out of here before we're butchered to death?"

"We're doing everything we can," said the black one.

"Really?" said Wally. "Because you were just sitting on your car, and it looked as if you were playing pat-a-cake."

"It helps us to concentrate," said the mulleted one. "Hey! Is that CGI Zombie #3210?" He pointed to the digital dead guy standing just behind Wally.

"I made that mistake earlier," Wally said, shaking his head. "No, this is #3021. #3210 is a complete asshole, apparently."

"Oh," said the mulleted cop. "Shame. I suppose it's right what they say. You should never meet your heroes."

"And in this case," Wally said, "you haven't."

Just then, from over by the concessions stand, there came a shrill squeal. Wally turned, saw Pigface making his way across the foyer with what looked like a dead goblin draped across his shoulder.

"Fuck this!" CGI Zombie #3021 said, and with that he walked straight through the glass door, ran across the parking lot, and didn't stop until he reached the McDonald's across the street.

"Wish we could do that," Ryan Phillipe said. "Actually…" He gave it a go. Nothing. Nothing but a smashed nose. "Worth a try," he said.

"Run!" said the eighties cops in unison.

Wally was already running, trying to keep as much distance between himself and Pigface as humanly possible. But Pigface didn't seem to be interested in him. The geriatric slasher only had eyes for Laurence R. Harvey and Ryan Phillipe. LRH had jumped up into Phillipe's arms now, the way Scooby used to do to Shaggy whenever they saw a masked janitor. From across the foyer, Wally was certain he could hear Phillipe's knees knocking together.

He didn't hang around to see what Pigface did to them. He ran all the way back to the maintenance closet, buried himself beneath a pile of dirty sheets, and prayed to the gods that those inept cops got him out of their alive.

He'd left a curry in the slow-cooker at home.

*

Pigface was drenched with blood. It slipped in through the slits in his mask; he could taste its bitterness. A coppery tang that reminded him, for some reason, of the first time he'd discovered his ma's box o' dildos.

For the longest time, he stood there breathless, just listening to the blood as it dripped from the head of his axe and pitter-pattered on the gaudy carpet beneath. He'd never killed a sprite before. Fuck knows who the other guy was, though. He looked familiar, but Pigface couldn't quite put his trotter on it.

Beyond the glass, the stereotypical eighties cops continued to throw up against the brickwork.

*

"Nope, nope, nope," said Ricks, wiping doughnut-vomit from his chin. Some of it had gotten into his mullet. He could hardly breathe. "I've never seen anything like that before in my life. Did you see the way that kid's head came away from his body? Then his arms and legs?"

Murtow's silvering stubble was caked with hundreds-and-thousands. "I recognised that kid from somewhere," he said. All that was left now was bile. He dry-heaved for a while.

"Really?" Ricks said. "What, like from a film, or something?"

Murtow nodded. "Nothing recent," he said. "*Hurghhhh*. I think… *hyergh*… I think he was famous, once upon a time."

"Well, not anymore, he's not," Ricks said. "We've got to get those people out of there. They're all going to die in there, Murtow. What the fuck is Dafoe up to?"

"Have faith, Ricks," said Murtow. "This is Willem Dafoe we're talking about. Willem Dafoe never lets anyone down."

"I thought that was Chuck Norris."

NINETEEN

The back doors which, it had been suggested, were always kept open so that theatre staff could pop out for a cigarette whenever it suited them, were just as magically shut as those at the front. These ones, however, were electrified. Billy Englund found this out the hard way, and had only recently picked himself up from the floor. His ginger hair was now wild; he looked less like Chucky and more like Carrot Top.

Willem Dafoe was trying to calm everyone down; the two girls—Marcia and Aretha—were hysterical. Freya, on the other hand, was doing everything she could do remain composed.

"We're never going to get out of here!" Aretha cried. "We're going to die! Pigface is going to get us!"

"Keep your voice down," Freya said. "There's no point losing your shit. If we do, we might as well just find that fucker and give him an easy target."

"I'd rather not," said Billy, pressing his hair down.

"Then we fight," said Freya. "This guy can be beaten. He was defeated in 2014, and again in 2015. There's no reason we can't take him down here."

"Freya's right," Dafoe said, raising his ice-cream scoop. "You have my scoop."

Freya nodded. It was a start, but if they were going to take down Pigface, they needed some real weapons. She turned to Billy. "There has to be something in this godforsaken place we can use to fight with," she said. "Dafoe's scoop is okay, but we want to kill this bastard, not tickle him."

Marcia stepped forward. The poor girl was shaking like a shitting pug, but she managed to speak. "What about the chainsaw? The one from *Texas Chainsaw Massacre: The Next Generation*? It's just down the hall in a display cabinet."

Dafoe sighed. "There's a good chance it's just a prop," he said. "And even if it's not, what are the odds it has fuel in it?"

"No, this is a good idea," Freya said. "Thanks, Marcia, is it?"

Marcia nodded.

"You did good," Freya said, smiling a little.

"Okay, so we get the chainsaw that may or may not be about as useful as tits on a fish, then what? We hunt down Pigface? He's smarter than that, not to mention the fact he's pretty good with an axe."

"We trap him," Freya said. "We trap him in one of the most inhospitable movies we can, and we leave him there to die."

"*The Shining*!" Billy said. "I mean, Shelley Duvall's been edited out of it, but it'll still be a pretty nasty place to get abandoned."

Freya nodded along. "It could work. We lead Pigface into The Shining, stay alive long enough for the starry vortex to appear, and, once we're out of there, someone pulls the plug up in the projectionist's booth. Shuts the movie down. Pigface spends the rest of his short life wandering the halls of The Overlook, being molested by gross old-lady ghosts."

Willem Dafoe tucked the ice-cream scoop into his belt. "It just might work," he said. "But what if the vortex doesn't appear in time. What if we can't get out of there before he kills us?"

"Then we join the ghosts of The Overlook," Freya said. "I've always wanted to take up ballroom dancing, anyway."

Billy leaned back against the hallway wall. "I never did like those creepy blue-dress twins," he said, staring off into nowhere. "But we're out of options. I say we do this.

We lead that prick to The Overlook and we strand him there."

"I really don't want to," Aretha said.

"Don't worry," Freya told her. "You and Marcia can be our projectionists. Barricade yourself in the booth and wait for us to come through the screen. Once we're through, shut the film down."

Marcia and Aretha nodded, seemingly happy with that arrangement.

"It's not much of a plan," Dafoe said, "but it's all we have. So we have to give it everything we've got." He went to unzip himself.

"Actually," Freya said, stopping his arm before it unleashed the Kraken, "this is one of those times where you're best off leaving your willy just where it is."

Dafoe looked a little disappointed, but Freya could see from his expression that he understood. "Maybe you're right," he said. "But let's just get something straight. We take down Pigface, it's coming out and I'm going to windmill all the way home."

"We kill Pigface," Freya said, "and you can do whatever you want with it."

Dafoe grinned. Freya thought, somewhat unceremoniously, she could fit at least two coins in the gap between his top front teeth.

"Then let's go snare us a pig-masked lunatic," Billy said.

"Amen," said Dafoe.

What an odd little gang we make, Freya thought. But hey, it worked for *The Dream Team*.

*

On a scale of one to ten, said the mask, *would you recommend this convention to fans of the genre? One being a firm no and ten being a fuck yeah!*

"I'd give it an eight," said Pigface. "I mean, the staff aren't very helpful. I haven't seen a single redshirt since we got here. And the venue's a little too big, for my liking. A lot of walking around with very few kills between. Apart from that, can't really complain."

You do realise you have a dead goblin on your shoulder? I mean, I didn't want to say anything, but it's like if you get a fleck of spittle on your lip. It's only a matter of time before someone points it out.

"Thanks," Pigface said. He peeled the goblin remains from his shoulder and threw them against the hallway wall. They stuck there for a moment—between a poster advertising *Saw XII* and one announcing the imminent arrival of *Bridget Jones's Menopause*—before sliding slowly downwards, leaving a trail of goblin blood and mucus in their wake. "You think I should go check on Ma? She's been sleeping for a while now. It'd be a shame for her to miss the end."

Far be it from me to make a suggestion, said the mask, *but wouldn't you be better off with her out of the way? She's a pain in the arse at the best of times. Just think how much you can achieve while she's kipping.*

Pigface thought about it. The mask, for once, was absolutely right. Ma might have been entirely responsible for this third, and somewhat belated, instalment, but that didn't mean she deserved a bigger part. A cameo. That's what she was. A fortuitous cameo. Like Bill Murray in *Zombieland* or Matt Damon in *Interstellar*. Sure, she'd advanced the plot a little, but she was no Maggie Smith.

At the end of the hallway, a sudden movement stopped Pigface dead. It was one of those sonsofbitches from the last movie he'd been sucked into. The little guy, rushing from left to right, from one screen to another.

Pigface smiled. "I see you, little one!" he said. The axe felt good in his hand. An extension of himself.

What are you talking about? asked the mask.

Pigface began to walk again. There was no point running; slowly, slowly, catchy midget. Besides, like most people—Sharon Osborne and Nicole Kidman excluded—he wasn't as young as he used to be. "Didn't you see it? Little guy, just ran across the hall down there?"

Didn't see a thing, said the mask. *But to be honest, I was looking the other way.*

"You're on my head," Pigface said. "Shouldn't you be looking the same way I'm looking?"

Well I was miles away, corrected the mask. *I was thinking, if I could be any other mask, what would I be? Quite fancy having a go as one of the dead presidents from Point Break.*

Just then, another shape darted across the hallway, this time from right to left. It wasn't the little guy this time; Pigface recognised the girl. The sound of a door whispering shut on its hydraulic hinges drifted along the hallway.

I saw that one! said the mask. *What are they doing? Don't they realise they're about to be murdered to death? This isn't the time to be playing silly buggers.*

"I don't know," Pigface said. He'd slowed down a little. They were up to something, and they were relying on his stupidity in order for whatever it was to work. He didn't like it one bit, for he was used to having the upper hand. Most of the kids he killed were dumb jocks and comely girls; usually they were the type of kids to put M&Ms in alphabetical order. The type of kids to think Tupac Shakur was a Muslim holiday. The type of kids to study for a blood test and still fail.

Occasionally—and it had happened once or twice over his inexhaustible career—he found himself going head-to-head with a smarter adversary. And whenever that happened, bad things came as a result.

You're not scared, are you? The mask was trying to wind him up. Trying and succeeding.

"Look," Pigface said. "I've *been* to Hell. Twice now. You don't know what it's like down there. I once spent a month stuck behind a tractor. A whole month just riding on this tractor's ass, and whenever I tried to overtake it would move right across with me. Did you know that in Hell, every homeless guy you ignored in life gets to spit in your mouth? Satan's a dick. A bigger dick than people give him credit for. So yes. I am being careful, because I don't want to end up back there behind that tractor, or having Henry the Hobo hawking into my throat. It's no fun. No fun at all."

Like a Yoko Ono concert? said the mask.

"A what?" Pigface asked.

But before the mask had chance to respond, there came a noise from the end of the hallway.

Riddingdingdingdingdingdingdingding—cough—ing-ding-ding. It sounded like someone making chainsaw noises. Bad chainsaw noises.

Pigface, for the first time that day, felt extremely vulnerable. He had no idea if his mother's shit Latin had given him immortality, and he wasn't about to find out the hard way.

Ridingdingdingdingdingding… on and on and on. And then a man stepped from an ingress halfway along the hallway. In his hand, a filthy chainsaw. It looked very real to Pigface, although the chain wasn't moving.

"Willem Dafoe," Pigface said. "Didn't Ma stick an axe in your back?"

Dafoe nodded and grinned that semi-evil grin of his. Pigface thought, *I could fit at least two coins in that gap.* "You can't kill Willem Dafoe," Dafoe said.

I thought that was Sydney Poitier, said the mask.

"That chainsaw's not even real," Pigface said, pointing at it with his axe, which was *very* real. "The chain's not going around."

Dafoe frowned and took a few steps toward Pigface. "It works just fine," he said. "*Riddingdingdingdingdingding—*"

"That's *you!*" said Pigface. "You're making shit chainsaw noises to make me think it's real."

"No I'm not."

"Yes you are. I can see your tonsils moving through that gap in your teeth."

"No you can't."

"Yes I can. You're trying to trick me. Larry Travers wasn't born yesterday, you know."

Technically you were born today, said the mask.

Pigface ignored it. "You think I'm stupid," he said to Dafoe.

"Aren't you?"

"Well I'm not the one making chainsaw noises whilst holding a chainsaw that doesn't actually work," Pigface said.

"It'll still hurt if I throw it at you," said Dafoe.

"Not as much as this axe," Pigface countered. He was no longer fearful of Willem Dafoe, who had now pulled what appeared to be an ice-cream scoop from his belt. "What's that?"

"It's a gun," Dafoe said.

"No it's not," said Pigface. "It's an ice-cream scoop."

"No it's not. It's a special gun."

"Are you on drugs?"

"Some," said Dafoe. "Now freeze! I don't want to have to use this, but I will."

Will you just kill this fucktard already? enquired the mask.

Pigface squeeed, and a second later he took an ice-cream scoop to the eye-socket. It hit him with such force that he staggered backward, his head fuzzier than a muppet's groin. It seemed he had severely underestimated the ice-cream scoop. The mask said as much.

You severely underestimated—

"I know!" said Pigface, shaking away the feeling of nebulousness washing over him. "Jesus! That smarted like a sonofabitch!" He could feel blood dripping down the side of his nose. Willem Dafoe had very nearly knocked his head off with a kitchen utensil.

When the haziness cleared a few seconds later, Pigface was livid. "That," he said, "was callous…" But he trailed off, because Willem Dafoe was halfway down the hall. The fake chainsaw lay on the carpet where Dafoe had been standing a moment ago.

He's only gone and done a runner, said the mask.

"Do you have to narrate everything?" Pigface said, spitting blood onto the carpet. "I mean, I'm not an idiot. I can see he's done a runner because I'm looking at him right now. Running."

Just trying to help—

"Well keep your mouth shut, yeah? That'd be a great help." Pigface began to follow Dafoe, who turned right into one of the screens along the way. "We've got him now," he said, somewhat optimistically. "Or my name's not Larry Travers. And it is."

*

Meanwhile, outside a helicopter hovered. Its blades moved so fast—they have to, you see, otherwise it'd just fall out of the sky—that Ricks's mullet almost detached from his head and scarpered across the parking lot like a stray chinchilla.

"I'm too old for this shit," said Murtow.

"What, helicopters?" Ricks said.

"No, this," replied Murtow, holding out a twelve-piece jigsaw puzzle. "It says 3-8 on the side."

"Shame," said Ricks. "I'd have loved to see it finished."

"Me too, Ricks," Murtow said, solemnly tossing the jigsaw puzzle onto the back seat. "Me too."

The helicopter came down slowly—they have to, you see, otherwise thee ground comes up too fast to meet them—and landed at the centre of the parking lot. Ricks and Murtow wasted no time; this was there chance to get into the multiplex and put a stop to this madness before it got any worse. They ran across to the chopper—so-called because the man who invented the helicopter, Harry Copter (Heli was his middle name), once used its rotors to slice up his Sunday vegetables—and climbed in.

"Take her up," Ricks told the pilot.

"As opposed to?" replied the sassy sonofabitch in the front seat. Without waiting for a reply, he hit the collective and pushed forward on the cyclic, and the chopper took to the air.

Beside Ricks, Murtow started to look a little peaky. His usually jet-black moustache had started to sprout whites, and he pouched his mouth, as if to keep something in.

"You okay?" Ricks asked. "You look terrible. Like James Earl Jones sucking an aniseed ball."

Murtow shook his head. "I've never flown before," he said.

"Me neither," called the pilot from the front seat. "I hope this thing has an ejector seat."

Ricks frowned, for an ejector seat on a helicopter was about as functional as an ashtray on a motorcycle or Stevie Wonder's sunglasses.

"He's just joking," Ricks assured Murtow.

"I'm not," said the pilot. "This is the highest I've ever been. Look at those buildings down there! They look like… like small buildings!"

"I don't want to die, Ricks," Murtow said, latching onto his partner's hand and giving it a tight squeeze. "If this thing goes down, I want you to take care of my wife and kids."

"Well, I'll do Tish and your oldest daughter," Ricks said, "but I draw the line at the boys and your seven-year-old girl."

Murtow frowned. "I didn't mean—"

"If this thing goes down," Ricks said, "I'm pretty certain we'll both be mangled beyond all recognition. People rarely survive helicopter crashes. They usually get all mushed up so that only a dentist can identify them. That's why they call them choppers."

"Actually," said the pilot. "Arnold Schwarzenegger coined the term 'chopper' in *Predator*. Before that they were known simply as 'windmill planes'."

"Ricks," whispered Murtow. "I don't think this guy knows what he's doing."

Ricks nodded. "I thought that when I saw the blind man's cane on the front passenger seat."

"I'm too old for this shit," said Murtow.

Somehow—and Ricks put it down to blind luck (pun intended) rather than skill—the pilot managed to land on the roof of the multiplex.

"That'll be twelve dollars," said the pilot.

"What?" Ricks was confused. "I thought you were a police helicopter?"

"Nope," said the pilot, tapping at the fare display. "Uber."

Murtow fished around for the money and paid the man. Six dollars. He was blind, after all. It was rude not to take advantage.

As they climbed out of the chopper, and as it took the skies once again, Ricks said, "You don't suppose he was *really* blind, do you?"

"Nah," Murtow said. "I think he was just trying to put the shits up us. Uber wouldn't allow a blind person to fly a heli—"

A sudden explosion cut him off mid-sentence, and then a rotor whipped through the air a few feet away before burying itself in a wall. The helicopter had smashed into the side of an adjacent building—a fire-extinguisher shop, of all things—and had burst into flames. Fortunately, the flames went out before they even had a chance to get going. Unfortunately, the pilot's head was already off by that point. At least there was something for the dentist to work with.

Ricks turned to Murtow and said, "It's one of those days today, isn't it?"

Murtow nodded. "On the bright side, it can't possibly get any weirder."

They ran across the rooftop toward the skylight at its centre. A metre square, and almost completely opaque, it was just big enough for them to fit through. But first they had to get the damn thing open.

"Do you have one of those clever little glass-cutter thingies?" Murtow said. "If we cut a tidy little circle, then slowly lift out the glass, we should—"

"CANNONBALL!" Ricks cried, and then he was flying through the air, his mullet flapping behind him like one of those signs—**WILL YOU MARRY ME, FANNY?**—they drag behind biplanes.

Murtow managed to get out of the way just in time. Ricks, now a tight ball of retardation, crashed through the glass and dropped into the multiplex foyer. He hit the concessions stand, bounced once or twice before thumping to the carpet.

It hurt a lot, but Ricks tried not to let it show. He staggered to his feet, one of which was now pointing in the wrong direction, and called up to Murtow, "Come on! It's not that far a drop."

"Your foot's on backwards," Murtow said, trying to keep his voice down.

Ricks looked down at it, saw that it was twisted right the way around, and said, "It's just a sprain. Come on, Murtow, time is of the essence."

"I'm too old for this shit," Murtow said, lowering himself carefully in through the aperture.

While his partner figured out a safe way down (there wasn't one), Ricks slammed his ankle against a wall; it snapped back the right way.

There was a meaty thud, and when Ricks turned around he saw that Murtow had finally decided to join him. "See," he said, as his partner peeled himself up from the carpet. "Told you it wasn't too bad."

Murtow was winded. "You did," he grunted. "You're an asshole."

Ricks drew his handgun and assumed The Crouch, that well-known position adopted by FBI agents just before they enter the ramshackle house of a serial killer. Ricks was good at The Crouch. Murtow was not. Murtow assumed The Lopsided Stoop, the not so well-known position assumed by drunken jockeys after climbing off a three-legged stallion.

"Let's do this," said Ricks, scuttling across the foyer like a crab with crabs.

Murtow followed. It was clear he was far too advanced of years for such silliness.

TWENTY

Once they were all in the auditorium, they separated. Billy Englund backed slowly up the first set of steps while Freya took the second. Willem Dafoe remained down at the front, where he would attempt to lead Pigface away from the others.

This has to work, Freya thought. *It has to!* But of course, it didn't have to work. Not really. There was nothing saying it would, no guarantees that anything would go accordingly. After all, things seldom did. The plan, if you could call it that, was not the greatest. There were so many factors out of their own hands, so many things they were relying on to happen, with no way of manipulating them. Basically, they needed a little bit of luck. In other words, not only were they up Shit Creek without a paddle, but the kayak they were in was made of live crocodiles and Shit Creek flowed directly toward Hell.

No sooner had they took up their positions than Pigface was in the room, squealing and jabbering to himself like a man possessed. When he saw them, he said, "I knew you fuckers were up to something. So, what it is? You have some kind of trap set? Am I about to be bashed about the snout by a swinging paint can? Huh?" He took a step toward Dafoe. "You," he said, pointing at the actor. "I'm going to kill you last. You're going to wish you'd never crossed me, Dafoe, you zany sonofabitch. I'm going to hurt you so much, you'll wish you were anyone else but you. Kathy Bates, OJ Simpson, Nicolas Cage… anyone!"

Freya stared up at the screen to see a car winding through the valleys, accompanied by an ominous orchestral score. The film had gone back to the beginning. Or perhaps Marcia and Aretha had figured out how to reset the thing.

Why would they do that?

But then Freya understood the thinking behind it. The girls were giving them as much time as possible to get out of there in one piece—a full two hours and forty minutes in this Director's Cut—for they still didn't know what would happen should they be stranded.

Clever girls, Freya thought.

Pigface turned to face her. "You must be the final girl," he said, sniffing at the air as if someone had dropped an eggy one.

"It wasn't me," said Billy.

"I know it wasn't," Freya said. "It was me. Sorry." To Pigface she said, "Can you stop sniffing it? You're starting to weird me out."

Pigface grunted. He said, "So this is it, then. The final battle. The denouement. The last scene." He turned to Willem Dafoe and raised his axe. "That does not mean there's still time to whip your tackle out, Dafoe."

Willem Dafoe visibly deflated and took his hand away from his crotch.

Ambling casually across the front row, exuding more confidence than Jen Soska at a Sylvia Soska lookalike contest, Pigface was the epitome of evil. "It's been an absolute pleasure hunting you down today," he said. "I haven't had this much fun since the seventies."

Freya turned her attention to the screen again. Jack Nicholson was talking to an empty passenger seat while Danny Lloyd perched dangerously between in the rear. They had edited Shelley Duvall out, and redubbed Nicholson's lines so it seemed he was conversing with his son, and not his now-absent wife.

Why is nothing happening? Freya thought. Why wasn't the movie claiming them, the way *Labyrinth* had?

"Of course," Pigface went on. "Things were a lot different in the seventies. Violence and gore was easier to get away with back then. Not like nowadays. You're only allowed to show one or two grisly killings an hour, the rest have to be implied. It's a fucking joke, if you ask me."

To her left, Billy was becoming agitated. He too was concerned about the lack of magical activity coming from the screen.

"… on the bright side, we're seeing more violence than ever before," Pigface said. "So that's something, at least. Anyway, I'm rambling on. What's say we get the butchering started, hm?"

He turned and began to climb the steps toward Billy, who was, by now, crying the tiniest tears Freya had ever seen. They were, she imagined, the same size as rat's tears, should a rat ever stump its toe against a piece of recalcitrant furniture.

"There's no need to cry, little man," Pigface told Billy, mockingly. "It'll all be over in a jiffy, and then those of us that aren't brutally dismembered can go on with our lives and put this whole nasty business behind us."

"Leave him alone!" Freya said, moving sideways along the row and banging her knees against the seats in front with every step she took. "Pick on someone your own size!"

Pigface squealed with delight. "I'm indiscriminate!" he said. "It doesn't matter to me if you're tall, short, fat, thin, religious… did I say short?"

Billy nodded and wiped the tears from his eyes. "You did. Twice."

The Torrances—minus the annoying one—had arrived at The Overlook and were currently being given the grand tour by its manager.

And still no magic interdimensional travel vortex. *You watch*, Freya thought. *Two will show up in a minute. Always the way.*

"I'm going to enjoy this," said Pigface. He now had Billy pegged into a corner, had already begun to swing his axe when—

There came a deafening blast, and something pinged off the head of Pigface's axe. "Freeze!" two men cried in unison.

Freya glanced through the semi-darkness of the theatre, could just make out the shapes of two crouching men down near the exit ramp. Well, one of them was crouching; the other was doing The Lopsided Stoop.

It was a pair of eighties cops. Freya recognised the mullet almost immediately, and the combination of sensible black cop and not-quite-with-it white cop was unmistakeable.

Pigface turned around and lowered the axe. "Did someone just shoot at me?"

The mulleted cop held up a hand. "That was me," he said. "Next time, it'll be right in your scrotum. Now drop the damn axe before I have to do something that will result in me seeing a police psychiatrist for years to come, only to be told that there's no saving me. I won't mind, though, because the psychiatrist will be a MILFy blonde, and those are right up my street, if you know what I mean. Did I ever tell you I had sex with Patsy Kensit?"

The black cop gave the mulleted cop a gentle nudge: *not now.*

"So you managed to get in," said Pigface to the cops. He had seemingly forgotten all about Billy and, once he was far enough away, Billy ran across to where Freya now stood, nursing her sore chair-battered knees.

"We did," the white cop said. "It's over, snoutboy. Throw down the axe or I'll blow you to kingdom come."

Pigface slowly descended. "Didn't you get the memo?" he said, opening up his body. "You can shoot me all you like. I can't be killed here in this world."

As if to test the theory, the black cop shot Pigface twice in the abdomen. Pigface staggered back with each hit but, other than that, he was unhurt.

"I'm too old for this shit!" cried the black cop.

"Me too!" said the mulleted one. "I mean, I'm not as old as Murtow here, but for this shit, I'm *definitely* too old."

Pigface *squeeed* and began taking the steps two at a time, axe arcing through the air. For an old guy he was reasonably lithe. Perhaps the film-world had reinvigorated him, made him new again. And why not? It had ostensibly rendered him immortal, after all.

The cops began to shoot; the theatre lit up with each report. Pigface was almost upon them when…

TWENTY-ONE

For a moment there, Freya had shut her eyes. Though she and law-enforcement had not always seen eye to eye, she didn't fancy bearing witness to the mutilation of a couple of buddy detectives. And so she had closed her eyes and prayed to the gods for a miracle.

Unfortunately, several of the gods were off playing golf, but at least one had stayed behind to keep an eye on things.

For when she opened her eyes, she was standing in a hotel foyer. Holidaymakers were checking out, skis tucked beneath one arm and luggage hanging from the other. It was colder than a witch's tit in that reception area. Freya wished she'd worn two pairs of socks that morning.

Too late now.

Someone bumped into her and she turned. It was Jack Nicholson, being led through the hotel by its manager— a wiry little fellow wearing a blue suit and what had to be a toupee. Danny was being dragged off to another part of the hotel by Dick Hallorann, the hotel's cook, played here by Scatman Crothers.

"I'll be damned," Freya mumbled. "It worked."

She looked around the reception area, searching for her fellow survivors, but they were nowhere to be seen. She didn't recognise any of the people milling around here. Pretty soon they would all be gone, their movie-world vacation at an end. Surely there were better hotels—less haunted hotels—in the near vicinity?

Freya watched the receptionist, waiting for the most opportune moment to slip past. A woman dressed in more clothes than were in Freya's entire wardrobe sidled up to the counter and began the process of checking out.

Without wasting a second more, Freya rushed by the counter, not even looking back to see if she'd been clocked.

She had to find Billy and Willem.

The second part of their shit plan was now in motion.

*

Billy recognised the brown-orange-and-red carpet the moment he landed face down upon it. For some reason the gods had decided to drop him from a great height on this occasion. Maybe the usual gods were out playing golf or something, Billy thought, leaving just one arsehole in charge of things.

He picked himself up from the carpet and stared along the hallway. This was The Overlook, all right. Doors were staggered off the hallway all the way to its end; the carpet was already giving him a fucking migraine.

"Freya?" he whispered. And then a little louder. "Dafoe?"

Nothing.

Great, Billy thought as he slowly walked along the hallway. *Whose idea was this again? Let's drop ourselves into one of the creepiest movies ever made. Oh, and while we're at it, let's take one of the most prolific serial killers of all time with us.* What a ridiculous idea, made even more ridiculous by the fact that someday, someone would probably write a novel about it.

Billy turned the corner at the end of the hallway and stepped into an identical one. *It would be so easy to get lost here,* he thought. *This is even more of a labyrinth than the actual fucking Labyrinth.*

He was about to start walking when something crashed into his ankle. "Fuck! Ah! Cock!" He hopped around on one foot, rubbing at the ankle of the other, and that was when he noticed the little boy. Dressed in denim dungarees and red sweater, and sitting upon a tricycle, the boy regarded Billy the way one might regard a purple turd or a truthful politician. "Little shit! You almost broke my shagging ankle! What are you doing, anyway? Speeding around the corridors on your own on that thing? Don't you know this hotel his haunted to fuck?"

The boy frowned. Then he held up his finger and started to talk to it. "Is this a sprite, Tony?" he said in a strange croaky voice. "A leprechaun?"

Billy fought the urge to kick the shit out of the kid right there and then. "Put your finger down, son," he said, finally putting some weight on his ankle. "Seriously. Don't you know talking to your finger is the first sign that you're a fucking idiot?"

The boy shook his head.

"Well it is," Billy said. "Now, I know who you are. You're Danny, aren't you? Your parents call you Doc?"

The boy nodded.

"Where's your dad, Doc?" Billy said, for the last thing he wanted was a chance encounter with a hyped-up axe-wielding lunatic. He'd had enough of that for one day already.

"He's downstairs, throwing a ball against a wall," Danny said. "He should be typing, but I think the ribbon's bolloxed."

Billy nodded. He didn't want to tell the kid too much about what was about to happen over the next couple of days, but at least the poor whippersnapper didn't have Shelley Duvall going mental around him as well as Jack Nicholson.

"Say, Doc?" Billy said, jovially. "You haven't seen a girl around here, have you?"

Danny's face contorted with fear. *He's a good actor, this lad,* Billy thought. *Don't know why he ended up as a pig-farming science-teacher in the Midwest.* "Two," he gasped. "Blue dresses. They want me to play with them. Forever. And ever. And—"

"No, this girl is older," Billy said. "Older and a lot prettier."

Danny shook his head. An abundance of 1980s hair danced around his ears. "Sorry," he said. "I'll keep an eye out for her, though."

Billy thanked him. It was pointless asking the kid if he'd seen Willem Dafoe, so he said his goodbyes and they went in opposite directions.

Only for the little dick to crash into Billy's other ankle less than thirty seconds later.

*

Willem Dafoe had never seen a hotel room like it. Stunning, it was. Not a thing out of place. A fully-stocked minibar. Wooden hangers in the wardrobe, not those cheap plastic ones. He made a mental note to leave a positive review on Trip Adviser before slipping into the bathroom. "Freya?" he said.

For some reason, they had been separated. He was all alone here. Apart from a tiny moth fluttering around a lampshade, the bathroom was also empty.

He turned to leave.

"Hey!"

Startled, Dafoe turned around, wishing now more than ever that he'd held onto his ice-cream scoop just a little longer.

There, sitting in the bathtub which had been empty only a second ago, was one of the most beautiful women Dafoe had ever seen.

"Did you just say something?" Dafoe asked her.

The woman shook her head.

"You did," he said. "You said 'Hey!'."

"Don't you fancy me?" said the woman pushing herself up to standing. Hot water steamed from her back, her breasts, and the thick dark thatch between her legs.

"I do," Dafoe said. "But I've seen the movie, I know how it turns out. If you could just stay over there, and don't go all mouldy granny on me, I reckon I could rub one out."

The woman stepped out of the tub; her face solemn and beautiful and still a little soapy.

As she took a step toward Dafoe, he said, "Seriously. I'm warning you. One more step and I'll punch your tits off."

"I won't turn into the old lady," said the woman. "Promise. Just come over here and kiss me."

"Look, lady, I've done tonnes of things I'm not proud of in my lifetime. Did you ever see *Speed 2: Cruise Control?*"

The woman shook her head.

"Well, it was appalling. So bad. And the only thing that could possibly equal that, in terms of sickness-inducing horror, is making out with a ghost I know to actually be a toothless hag."

"*Look* at me," said the woman. "See how *hot* I am?"

"*Now!*" Dafoe said. "Soon as the tongue goes in, the teeth come out. I know how it goes, so thanks, but no thanks."

The beautiful woman looked suddenly disconsolate. Dafoe felt bad; worse than he'd felt making Mr Bean's Holiday. "Okay," he said. "We can do it, but if you witch out on me it's going to be a boner-killer."

The woman grinned.

Twenty seconds later, Willem Dafoe rushed from the hotel room, his pants around his ankles and his semi-on slowly shrivelling. "What did I tell you?" he called back over his shoulder. He slammed the door shut, yanked his pants up, and sighed. "Three more seconds," he said. "That's all I needed."

He began walking along the hallway. "Freya?" he called out. "Billy?"

Back in the room he'd just left, the ghost-hag cackled and cackled and, because she was getting on a bit, pissed all down her spectral leg.

*

Ricks and Murtow had spent the last five minutes discussing the interdimensional travel, a subject neither of them knew too much about. Still, they gave it a whirl, and it turned out that they knew even less than they initially thought.

"So we're in the film?" Murtow said, with a modicum of uncertainty. "We've crossed dimensions and now we're trapped in a Stanley Kubrick movie?"

Ricks holstered his gun—there was no one around to shoot anyway—and said, "How else do you explain this?" He motioned to the hotel all around them. They were standing in a hallway. A sign just in front of them, seemingly announcing the unwinding hours, read THE GOLD ROOM. "It's The Overlook, Murtow. I'll bet there's a fucking maze outside, a Snowcat in the garage, and a naked witch in Room 237."

Murtow still looked unconvinced, even though he was surrounded by evidence. "So where is everyone?"

"They all left," Ricks said. "At the start of the film everyone pisses off and leaves the Torrances to their own devices. I'll bet there ain't ten people left in this whole hotel, and we're two of 'em."

"Tish is going to kick my ass, Ricks," Murtow said. "I knew something bad was going to happen. As soon as that call came in, I just knew it was going to go south.

We should have left it for Jack Breacher. He loves this kind of shit."

Shaking his head, Ricks said, "Breacher's a cock. And just think about it. We put Pigface in a body-bag, we'll be captains come sun-up." He was excited. He hadn't been this excited since he traded his trailer in for a bigger trailer.

"Okay," Murtow said. "Suppose you're right. We're in the film. Somehow. Now what?"

Ricks was about to answer when suddenly a voice came from THE GOLD ROOM. A male voice. An unhinged male voice.

Ricks drew his weapon. It was a lethal weapon, as many of them are. He dropped into The Crouch™ (other stances are available) and shuffled along the hallway, back to the wall.

Murtow dropped into The Lopsided Stoop and crab-walked across to Ricks. "This is a bad idea, Ricks," he said.

"On three," Ricks said. "One… two…"

Of course, he never reached three. Every single time they went on two. Sometimes, just to piss Murtow off, Ricks would go on one. On this particular occasion he went on two-point-two.

"Freeze!" he said to the guy sitting at the unmanned bar. His red ochre corduroy jacket gave him away; the axe leaning against the wood panelling of the bar was another clue.

If Jack Torrance heard him, he didn't show it, simply sat there, sipping nothingness from a dusty glass and rambling to no one in particular.

Ricks approached slowly, not wanting to startle the guy. He had an axe, after all. Halfway across the ballroom, Murtow latched onto his arm.

"I've seen this movie," he said. "That dude ain't right. We should back the fuck out of here before he sees us."

But Ricks wasn't listening. He'd always wanted to meet Jack Nicholson, so there was no way he was going to pass up the opportunity now. "Look, we've got guns," he said, holding his up as proof. "If he starts getting all psycho, rambling on about caretakers and suchlike, we'll put a bullet in him. None of this is real, Murtow. Remember that. Think of it as a virtual reality game."

"Except we could *die* here," Murtow said. "In fact, there's a damn good chance we will. *Especially* if you go up and poke that bear." He nodded in the direction of Jack Torrance, who was now removing notes from his wallet in order to pay for his imaginary drink.

"We need to find those others," Ricks said. "And this dude knows his way around this place. I'm just going to ask him a few questions and we'll be on our way."

Murtow sighed. "Okay, but then we're out of here."

"That's what I said," Ricks said. He turned and walked across to the bar, settling himself down on the stool next to Jack Torrance. He kept his police-issue handgun trained upon the guy at all times. Jack didn't even notice he was there until he spoke. "Mr Torrance?"

Jack looked up, a crazed smile playing about his face. His eyebrows were so far up his face that Ricks was sure they could be reclassified as a fringe. "Ah!" he said, seemingly delighted Ricks had joined him. "*More* ghosts. Care for a drink, you sonofabitch? I like you. I've always liked you. Salt of the earth."

Ricks politely declined. He hadn't drunk air from an empty cup since his niece's fourth birthday party. Some picnic that fucking was. "I'm looking for some people," Ricks explained. "A girl, a midget thing, and Willem Dafoe. Also, there's a guy in a bloody white apron and a pig-mask knocking about. You might want to steer clear of that one. We're here to take him into custody, or shoot him, whichever is easiest."

"White man's burden," Jack said. "Have you met Lloyd here?" He signalled the empty space behind the bar. "Best goddamn bartender from Timbuktu to Portland, Maine… or Portland, Oregon for that matter."

"Yes, *Lloyd*," Ricks said, smiling at the empty space. "Great guy. Good to see you again, Lloyd. You're looking well." To Jack he said, "So you haven't seen anyone? Nobody has been in here?"

Jack shook his head. That was when he noticed what Ricks was holding. "Is that a real gun or a prop?"

"It's, erm, real," Ricks said, lowering it. "Alrighty then. Well, I guess we're done here. Say, your wife wouldn't have bumped into anyone, would she? While she's screeching around the hotel like a bug-eyed retard?"

"My wife's not here," Jack said. "This is the Director's Cut. Much nicer. A lot less whiny."

"Oh, that's a good idea," Ricks said as he climbed down from the stool. "Well, it was lovely meeting you. Loved you in Mars Attacks, by the way."

"No you didn't," Jack said.

"You're right," Ricks said. He made his way back to Murtow, who had already retreated to the door. "He hasn't seen anyone. Did you know this is the Director's Cut, now with a hundred-percent less Shelley Duvall?"

"That's a good idea," Murtow said. "So what now?"

"Now?" Ricks said. "We go hunt us down some swine."

"I'm far too elderly for these shenanigans," Murtow said.

*

Pigface couldn't believe how foolish he had been. Of *course* Dafoe, the midget, and the final girl were up to something; he'd known that. And yet he'd still followed them into the theatre. And now he was trapped in some hotel-based movie. It was so cold, and the décor was severely outdated.

This place sucks, said the mask. *Art Deco does my head in. Give me a good old Neo-Byzantine any day of the week. This hotel looks like Josef Hoffman came in, spunked all over the place, and then left.*

Pigface made his way toward an elevator. "Let's just find those assholes, kill them, and get the fuck out of here again," he said. "I mean, this is clearly a nice film. It's set in a posh hotel. I wouldn't be surprised if we didn't bump into Grace Kelly at some point." He pushed the button on the wall panel and took a step back. The needle began to shift from tight to left as the elevator descended through the levels. Pigface tapped his foot as he waited. He even whistled a little. "What's this film called again?"

The Shining, said the mask.

"Never heard of it," said Pigface. "But even the title suggests wonderful things. *The Shining.* Things that shine. Hm." The elevator beeped as it reached the ground floor. "Ah!" Pigface said. "Our carriage awaits."

The doors whispered open and Pigface took a step forward, but no more, for a wall of blood slammed into him like a tsunami of menstruation. It filled his throat, his ears, pretty much anything that wasn't plugged up. The force of it sent him sprawling back into the lobby, where he crashed into a beige sofa. The blood pooled outwards, stretching all the way to the entrance on the other side of the room.

Pigface lay there for a while on his back, staring up at the huge crystal chandeliers hanging from the ceiling.

What was that about Grace Kelly? asked the mask.

"Shut the fuck up."

TWENTY-TWO

Freya found Billy on the second floor, nursing injuries to both of his ankles. When he saw her emerge from the stairwell, he fairly lit up. Like a Christmas tree, albeit one of those miniature ones you put on your desk at the office.

"What happened?" she said, motioning to his ankles.

"Little shit on a tricycle," Billy said. "You know the one?"

Freya knew the one. "The finger-talker?" she said. "Redrum! Redrum! And all that bollocks." Billy nodded. "That kid was a good actor. Did you know that he ended up teaching science and farming pigs in the Midwest?" When Billy nodded again, she said, "The perils of being a child star, huh? I think the kid from *E.T.* grew up to be a prostitute on Hollywood Boulevard."

"No, I think she grew up to be Drew Barrymore," Billy said.

"Oh, yes! I think you're right. I always get those two confused."

They walked slowly along the hallway, occasionally calling out for Willem Dafoe. He was here somewhere; they could smell his willy. Like brie, it was. A cheap brie.

"Maybe we should head over to Room 237," Billy suggested. "That's the most famous room in the hotel."

"It was 217 in the book," Freya reminded him.

"Ah, Kubrick," Billy said. "Sure did make it his own, didn't he?"

So they made their way across to Room 237, hoping Dafoe had the same idea.

*

Dafoe found himself standing in some sort of boiler room. Machinery clicked and clacked all around him. Pipes hissed and whined as water passed through them. He had no idea how he'd arrived at his present location, but guessed he had taken a wrong turn in the stairwell somewhere.

He turned to leave.

"Freeze!"

Dafoe threw his hands up, and a little bit of his breakfast. When he saw the eighties detectives, he relaxed and lowered his hands. The mulleted cop lowered his weapon. It looked, Dafoe thought, like a lethal one. "You scared the shit out of me," he said, patting at his chest as if his breasticles were on fire.

The black cop stepped forward and extended his hand. Willem reached out and shook it. "Detective Murtow," the cop said. "And this is Ricks."

"Of *course* it is," Dafoe said, shaking Ricks's hand. "Willem Dafoe. Any sign of Pigface? Freya? Billy?"

"We haven't seen any of them," Murtow said. "This place is huge. We just got lost in the bathroom. Ended up in the ventilation ducts."

Ricks grinned. "It was awesome. I even took my shoes off and threw on a dirty white vest."

Dafoe didn't know whether they were fucking with him or not, and he didn't have time to press them further. "We've got to find that sonofabitch. We've got a plan."

"A plan?" Ricks said.

"It's a detailed proposal for doing or achieving something," Dafoe said.

"Oh," said Ricks. "And that would be?"

Dafoe made his way toward the door. "First we find Pigface," he said. "Ricks, put your shoes back on. Things are about to get messy."

*

Dafoe was not in Room 237. The pretty woman in there said he'd been by, but didn't stick around.

"Nice lady," Billy said as they left the room. "Good boobs."

"Can't say I noticed," said Freya. But she had noticed. "We need to get down to the ground floor. Wait for Dafoe in the lobby."

"And hope we don't bump into Pigface in the meantime," Billy said. "I don't know about you, but this place is really starting to give me the creeps."

"It's not real," Freya reminded him as they came to a halt in front of the elevator. She pushed the button to summon it and took a step back. "It's just a movie, and we're just tourists passing through. The only thing we need to fear here is Pigface. The rest of it is just special effects and smoke-and-mirrors."

"Mirrors are scary," Billy said, shuddering.

"I'll bet they are when you're staring into them," Freya said, nudging him playfully in the ear.

The elevator arrived and the doors opened to reveal a pair of creepy twins. Their blue dresses were splashed here and there with blood. Neither of them spoke.

"We'll take the next one," Freya said.

The elevator doors shut and it went on its way.

Billy had turned a brilliant shade of white.

"At least it wasn't a mirror," Freya said.

*

Pigface arrived at something called THE GOLD ROOM. A solitary man sat at the bar nursing an empty glass and talking to thin air.

Nope, the mask said.

Pigface agreed. He turned around and went back the way he came.

*

"… and that's how I ended up shagging Patsy Kensit," Ricks said. The story was so unbelievable that Dafoe took it with a pinch of salt. Murtow had spent the last ten minutes rolling his eyes and sighing; how many times had he had to hear that bullshit? South Africans and diplomatic immunity, indeed.

"Dafoe!"

There, standing in the lobby, Freya and Billy were a sight for sore eyes. And Willem Dafoe had *really* sore eyes, for the steam in the boiler room had fairly cocked up his vision.

"You have no idea how glad I am to see you guys," Dafoe said. "We thought you were dead."

"Not dead," Billy said.

Dafoe looked down at the little man. There was something not quite right about his hue. He looked ill. "You're the colour of Elijah Wood," Dafoe said. "Take it you've seen one of the hotel's many ghosts?"

"You could say that," Freya said. "Those freaky twins hijacked our elevator. You see anything creepy?"

Dafoe thought about the witch up in 237. He shook his head; he didn't want to come across as some kind of old pervert. "Nothing," he said.

"That's funny," said Freya. "Because we were just up in Room 237, and—"

"She tricked me!" Dafoe spluttered. "She's very tricky. Good boobs, too."

"Can't say I noticed," said Freya. But she had noticed. "Anyway, we shouldn't just stand here. We need to put our plan into action."

"What's the plan?" asked Murtow.

"It's a detailed proposal for doing or achieving something," Billy said.

"Can someone tie my shoelaces?" Ricks said, for he was struggling something terrible.

"Why did you take your shoes off?" Freya asked.

"Ventilation ducts," Murtow said.

"Oh," said Freya and Billy in unison.

All of a sudden, Jack Nicholson limped through the lobby. The axe in his hand looked heavy. He dragged one foot behind him. He looked manic.

"I'm not gonna hurt you," he said when he reached the foot of the grand staircase. "I'm not gonna hurt you. You didn't let me finish. I'm just gonna bash your brains in."

"Who's he talking to?" Dafoe asked.

"It's where his wife was edited out," Freya said, pointing to the empty staircase, which Jack was now climbing, swinging his axe at nothing in particular.

"But it doesn't make any sense," Billy said.

"No, but it's still better," Dafoe said.

Jack Nicholson reached the top of the staircase and then tottered unsteadily for a moment. The next thing, he was lying on his back at the bottom of the stairs, snoring like a walrus with a head cold.

"Anyway," Freya said, dismissing what had just happened as secondary and not in the least bit significant. "Where were we?"

Dafoe had the beginnings of a terrible headache. This was all too much to take. Just a few hours ago he had been acting opposite one of the great leading ladies of this generation—and the generation before it—and now *this*. You couldn't make it up.

"*Squeeeeeeeee!*"

It came from a corridor off the lobby. Pigface was close.

"Quick! Everyone get to the maze!" Freya said.

"To hell with that!" Ricks said. "I can't even tie my own shoelaces. What makes you think I'll be any good at navigating a hedge maze?"

"*Squeeeeeee!*"

"Second thoughts," Ricks said. "See you down there." And with that he took off, out through the front entrance and down toward the maze, kicking up snow and slush as he went.

"Don't tell me," Dafoe said to Murtow, who looked as if he might start crying at any moment. "You're too old for this shit?"

"*Way* too old," Murtow said. "Let's go."

Dafoe shook his head and patted Murtow on the back. "Someone has to stay behind. Someone has to lead him down to the maze."

"We talked about this," Freya said. "We decided *I'd* be the bait. I *am* the final girl, after all. If anyone can beat him, it's me."

Dafoe didn't want to hear it. There was no way he could allow Freya to place herself in danger like that. "Just run," he said. "I should have stopped this asshole from ever reaching reality. I have a chance to put things right."

"But—"

"*Squeeeeeee!*"

*

Pigface entered the lobby, saw them all standing there in one easily-accessible congregation, and *squeeed*. He couldn't believe his luck. He said as much. "Well kiss my genitals and call me unclean," he said. "Look at you all, just standing there waiting for me." He did a quick headcount, then said, "Where's the one with the mullet? You know what? It doesn't really matter." He raised his axe and began chopping them all to bits.

At least, he *would* have if they hadn't all run out of the hotel, screaming and yelling. Willem Dafoe stopped at the hotel entrance and gave Pigface the finger.

"You want us?" he said. "You're gonna have to work for it." And then he was gone, out into the blizzard with the rest of them.

Pigface marched across to the open door. It was torrential out there. Only an idiot would venture out sans suitable clothing.

Are you going after them? asked the mask. *You're not really dressed for it.*

Pigface stepped out into the freezing snow and began following the footprints down the embankment. "What's the worst that could happen?" he said.

And that, said the mask, *is why you keep dying.*

*

The maze was a masterpiece in design and execution. Its walls were high enough to stop cheaters from climbing over, and every now and then there was a wooden bench for lazy cunts to take a breather. It had more twists and turns than a M. Night Shamalamadingdong movie. In the Stephen King book, the topiary came to life; in the

Stanley Kubrick movie—the version they were currently living—the maze was thankfully deader than Alderaan.

They found Ricks, covered in snow, five minutes into the maze. He was pacing around at a dead end, babbling on about Patsy Kensit and hitting himself in the temple with his handgun.

Freya managed to calm him down and they continued toward the maze's centre.

"I'm worried about Dafoe?" Billy said, checking back over his shoulder. "Do you think Pigface got him?"

Freya sighed, her breath crystalizing in the air in front of her face. She should never have allowed Dafoe to play bait. Then again, there was always a slight chance she wasn't the final girl. In which case, God bless Willem Dafoe, for he might very well have just saved her life. "He'll catch us up," she said, more hopeful than anything.

They jogged through the maze, occasionally arriving at a dead end. When that happened, they had no choice but to backtrack. The snow at least allowed them to see from which direction they had just come.

Trouble was, it was snowing so heavily that their footprints were already beginning to disappear as they filled in with fresh snow.

Ten minutes from now, Freya thought, *and the prints will be gone for good. Shit! What if we never get out of here? What if we end up just like Jack Torrance? Sitting against a hedge, frozen stiffer than Michael Hutchence at an auto-asphyxiation convention?*

Off in the distance, Pigface squealed.

"We're too lost for this shit!" said Murtow.

He had a point.

*

You just had to do it, didn't you? chastised the mask. *Straight into the giant maze without a second thought. In a blizzard, of all things!*

"Will you pipe down?" Pigface said, shivering somewhat and dusting the snow from his shoulders. "It's just a maze. These things are never that difficult. Otherwise we'd be seeing dead bodies all around the place, wouldn't we?"

They turned right at a T-junction, and there, nestled against the edge of the maze, sat an ice-covered man. Pigface recognised him as the guy from THE GOLD ROOM. A bloody axe sat on the snow next to him.

"Probably for the best," Pigface said. "Nobody wants two axe maniacs running around out here. Could be terribly confusing."

He hasn't been out here long, said the mask.

"How do you know?"

There's barely any snow on him. Also, didn't we see him just an hour ago, jabbering to an invisible bartender?

"Good point," Pigface said. "Well, he's nothing to do with our plotline. Let's keep going. The sooner this is done, the sooner we can return to the theatre for Ma."

Whoopie-doo, said the mask. *Maybe we'll both get lucky and you'll die before then.*

*

Willem Dafoe raced through the maze, cursing every time he followed the footprints to a dead end. Those dickheads had made more wrong turns than Stevie Wonder at Brands Hatch.

Eventually he caught up to them. Freya, it seemed, was happy to see him. She threw her arms around him. "Shit, we thought you were dead!" she said, her breaths heavy and her words slurred.

"Not yet," Dafoe said as he led them toward the centre of the maze. "We need to make sure he's still following us, though. If those prints get filled in, he might not find us and this whole plan goes out the window."

"Maybe we ought to make sure that doesn't happen," Billy said.

Dafoe stopped for a second. He too was breathless and tired; the inclement weather was affecting them all, slowly sucking the life from them. "What you got in mind?"

*

Precisely three minutes later, Pigface turned a corner and saw the message.

"Cheeky bastards!" he said.

There, in the snow, one of them had pissed the words:

THIS WAY ASSHOLE

*

They arrived at the centre of the maze only to find there was nothing there. No bandstand. No water-feature. Not even a sign saying WELL DONE! YOU MADE IT! While Freya wasn't too disappointed, Ricks was losing his shit.

"Not even a sign!" he said, kicking up snow. "I mean, we could die out here, and there'll never be any proof we completed this fucking thing!"

"Calm down, Ricks," Murtow said. "It's just a maze."

"No," Ricks said. "It's *not* a maze. You know why, Murtow? Because mazes have signs at the centre, which this clearly FUCKING DOESN'T!"

"Everyone quiet!" Dafoe said. He had taken up position at the aperture they had just entered through and was keeping guard. "I think I hear him. He's close."

They all fell silent. At first Freya didn't hear a thing, but then she turned her head a few centimetres to the right, and caught the words, "… who pisses in the snow, anyway? I mean, really?"

"Everyone!" Dafoe said. "Over there. As soon as he comes around this corner, I'm going to twat him with… with…" He trailed off, bent down, picked something up from beneath the hedge, and said, "with this tiny stick."

"Not really a lethal weapon, is it?" said Ricks.

Dafoe inspected the twig. "It's got thorns on it," he said.

"You'd better scratch the shit out of him," Murtow said. "Otherwise we're all dead, and Tish'll kill me if I'm not back for dinner."

All of them, apart from Dafoe, scarpered to the other end of the clearing. Dafoe pushed himself as far into the hedge as he could and waited.

Freya made the sign of the cross over her heart and held her breath.

As far as breaths went, it wasn't the most fragrant.

*

Aretha and Marcia watched nervously from the relative safety of the projectionist's booth. Marcia's finger hovered over the big red button which would shut the movie down.

Now I know how Kim Jong-Un feels every day of the week, she thought.

They waited.

*

Pigface stepped into the clearing, and his first words were, "Not even a fucking sign? Really?" His second words were, "Agh! A thorny stick!" as Willem Dafoe lunged from the snow-covered hedge to his right and began scratching at his neck with the spiny twig.

"How do you like it, huh?" Dafoe said. "Not nice, is it? Not nice being the victim."

Pigface brought his axe up and clobbered Dafoe underneath the chin. A tooth—unsurprisingly a big one—flew from Dafoe's mouth and landed on the snow down by his feet. Unconsciousness threatened to claim him. It was all a bit uncertain for a few seconds. Dafoe knew that if he went down it would all be over. He'd be in a hundred pieces by the end of the hour.

He shook the fuzziness away and forced the thorny twig into one of the eye slits of Pigface's mask.

"Ow!" Pigface said, staggering backward. The snow crunched underfoot like the skulls of a thousand children—or perhaps something less morbid… vanilla meringue?

"Here!" someone called from the edge of the clearing.

Dafoe turned just in time to see Freya throw a handgun in his general direction. Ricks stood next to her, looking fairly confused at his suddenly empty holster.

When Dafoe caught the gun—and it took a while, because apparently the Wachowskis had filmed this scene—he said, "But bullets don't do anything to him!"

"Pistol-whip the fucker," Billy said, mining the act.

"Knock his block off!" said Freya.

"Do it *quick!*" Murtow said, checking his watch. "I might make it back for prawn cocktails."

Rushing across the clearing, Dafoe raised the handgun. Now would have been the time to say something witty, like James Bond did in his movies, but all Dafoe could come up with was, "Time to bring home the bacon," so he kept his mouth shut and just hit the fucker.

Pigface went down like a turd in a punchbowl. He grunted as he thumped into the snow. The axe slipped from his grasp, and Dafoe wasted no time in picking it up.

"I'm going to axe you a question," he said, and was about to bring the blade down when—

Pigface groaned, with both pain and embarrassment. "What was that? Was that supposed to be a *coup de grace* wisecrack?"

Dafoe nodded.

"You did it all wrong," Pigface said, nursing his wounded head but remaining on his back. "You've got to come up with something clever. Like… like, 'Time for pork chops!'." He nodded. "See? Because I'm Pigface, and you've got a big chopper in your hand."

He didn't want to admit it, but Dafoe was secretly impressed. "Cool," he said. "Time for pork chops!" and he went to bring the axe down when—

"You can't say it *now*!" Pigface said. "It's already been used. You'll have to come up with something else, otherwise you look like a fucking idiot."

Dafoe shrugged. "You're bacon me nervous?"

"There you go," Pigface said. "Now try to include the axe."

"When I'm done with you," Dafoe said, "you'll need more than just oinkment."

"Actually," Pigface said. "Kill me now so I don't have to hear any more of those."

Dafoe sighed, shrugged, and brought the axe down.

At the centre of the clearing, the swirling vortex of stars and magic appeared. Snow drifted into it. A few seconds later, so did two stereotypical 1980s detectives and a little fellow dressed as a Good Guys doll.

"Dafoe!" Freya called. She was right next to the portal, understandably anxious to get a wriggle on, before the thing closed up once again.

Dafoe turned and began sprinting across the snow, his feet sinking, slowing him down. Freya stepped through the portal; Dafoe saw it swallow her up.

He leapt just as the portal began to shrink.

TWENTY-THREE

Freya, Ricks, Murtow, and Billy stared anxiously up at the screen. Snow continued to drift into the theatre through it, only to melt a second later thanks to the auditorium's unattended heating system.

Dafoe leapt toward the screen, and while he was airborne Freya repeated over and over, "He's gonna make it. He's gonna make it."

"He's not gonna make it," Ricks said.

"I'm too old for this shit!" Murtow whispered.

Dafoe's face contorted (more than usual) as he moved through the air, and then he hit the screen. But instead of coming through it, he bounced off and landed on his ass in the snow.

"Told you," said Ricks.

*

Dafoe sat up, stared at the empty space where, just a second ago, there had been a portal, and said, "Well, that's fucked it."

Across the clearing, Pigface was laughing. "Didn't make it, huh?" he said, pushing himself up to a sitting position. "That's just… just one of the funniest things that could have happened."

Dafoe went across to where Pigface sat and plonked himself down. "Shut up, gammonhead."

Pigface chuckled. He leaned over and spat. Blood sprayed out through the mask's mouth slit and turned the snow crimson. "Why didn't you kill me?" he said. "I mean, you had the axe, you kinda had the witty words to despatch me by. Why didn't you finish me off?"

Dafoe shrugged. "Figured you were going to die here anyway," he said. "Seemed a bit cruel to put an axe in your head, just in case."

Pigface snorted. "Look at us," he said. "A couple of old wash-outs, about to freeze to death. Or starve to death, whichever comes first."

Dafoe's eyes lit up then, and yet the rest of his features seemed to darken. He squeezed the axe handle so tight that his red-cold knuckles turned white.

"What?" Pigface said. "Why you looking at me like that? Dafoe? What's with the grin?"

The maniac actor began to laugh.

*

"Well," Billy said. "At least he'll survive for a while. Pigface has plenty of meat on him. And did you see that lovely hat Dafoe fashioned out of Pigface's pubic hairs? Eat your heart out, Ed Gein."

Freya couldn't believe what she had just witnessed. Three times she had upchucked in the aisle. She hadn't been sick that many times during a film since *Notting Hill*.

*

Aretha and Marcia had upchucked seven times between them as Dafoe took Pigface apart with that axe. They hadn't been sick that many times during a film since the *Point Break* remake.

"What now?" Aretha asked.

Marcia looked down to the theatre floor. The girl, Freya, was trying to get their attention. When she saw that she now had it, she drew a finger across her throat: *Shut it down.*

Marcia pushed the big red button.

The massive screen went dark.

*

"Edie Travers?"

Edie opened her eyes. "Wha… where… who—"

"We're arresting you on suspicion of aiding and abetting a magically-reanimated felon. You have the right to remain silent. Anything you say can and will be used against you in a court of law. You have the right to an attorney—"

"Who the fuck are you?" she asked the mulleted one. "Where's my Larry?"

"Your Larry," said the other cop—who looked a lot like Danny Glover, back when Danny Glover still looked like Danny Glover—"is currently being eaten by Willem Dafoe. Some of him is being worn as a woolly hat. Tragic, I know, but what goes around comes around."

"Bugger," Edie said as Ricks slapped the cuffs on her. "Don't suppose inmates are allowed dildos in prison?"

*

Outside the multiplex, the parking lot was teeming with police and news vans. Freya, Marcia, Aretha and Billy were draped with those dirty brown blankets they give you when you've just been through the wringer.

"Well," Freya said, "I guess they'll make a movie out of this someday."

"Or someone will write a book about it," Billy said. "I won't be buying a copy, I can tell you that much."

"Doubt *anyone* will," Marcia said, winking at nothing in particular.

Ricks and Murtow emerged from the building; between them was the crone, Edie Travers. She was spitting venomous bile, but neither Ricks or Murtow seemed to be paying her any attention. They flung her in the back of a police car, high-fived one another, and then peeled away from the parking lot at a speed liable to take them back to the future.

They all stood in silence for a while, taking it all in, but then the silence became too much and Freya said, "Anyone want to go grab a drink?"

Billy nodded. "Sure," he said. "Can we go somewhere where they serve shorts?"

Nobody laughed.

And rightly so.

EPILOGUE
(Or the bit after all the other stuff's happened)

Manny Cinquetento slipped into the maintenance cupboard and pulled out a 40oz bottle of whiskey. It had been three weeks since FearFest, that fateful day in which hundreds of foolish kids had lost their lives.

Manny still counted his blessings he'd been given the weekend off. *That could have been me,* he often reminded himself. *All squashed up or chopped to pieces.* It really didn't bear thinking about it.

He took a few slugs from the bottle and moved through the semidarkness to where he kept his booze. His first day back was going well, thus far. Thankfully, he had a decent buzz on. It sure did help things move more smoothly.

He pulled the sheet away from his stash and—

"Please don't kill me!"

Manny's heart jumped into his throat, for there, eating what appeared to be one of his own arms, hunched the emaciated form of Wally Perkins.

Manny did what any good maintenance man would upon discovering a self-cannibalising former event organiser.

He slowly backed out of there, walked out of the building, changed his name by deed poll, became a paediatrician, married an ex-prostitute, had three kids and sold one to Madonna, and later died of a heart-attack following a binge on far too much cocaine for human consumption.

It wasn't a bad life.

SECOND EPILOGUE
(When one is just not enough)

2125 – USS Reacharound – Somewhere just outside the Germani Sphere

"Captain Kane?" Zelda said, knocking on his sector door. For a synthetic she was pretty hot. Kane had often thought about stripping her down and giving her a damn good oil job.

"What is it, Zelda?" Kane asked. Bearded, heavy-set, and wearing just a pair of dirty long-johns, Captain Lucius Kane looked just like every other captain in the fleet. Some had grey beards, some brown, but if you didn't have a beard you could never expect to become a captain. The long-johns were just for show.

Zelda cleared her throat—and it was a throat Kane wanted to investigate more fully, when time allowed—and said, "There has been some… *progress* on PF78."

Kane stood from his desk. His erection knocked over one of those desk tidies. Pencils, paperclips, and rulers of various shapes and sizes spilled onto the floor. "What kind of progress?" he said.

PF78—named after Pigface and the year of his official retirement—was the ship's whole point for existing.

Zelda paused for dramatic effect, walked across to where Kane stood, and placed a hand upon his shoulder. "They've done it, Captain," she said. "They've finally managed to correct the algorithms."

"And there are no side-effects?" Kane said, breathless with excitement. "No extra heads or anything this time?"

Zelda shook her own head. "He's perfect, Captain," she said, smiling that beautiful artificial smile of hers. "Just like we knew he would be."

From somewhere off in the distance—the laboratory in Sector Twelve, Kane guessed, since that was where they were working on him—there came a hellish *squeee*.

"I'll be damned," Kane said. "Say, Zelda, let's have a shag to celebrate."

THE END